Vignettes

Vignettes

By
Daniel Soha

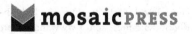

Library and Archives Canada Cataloguing in Publication

Title: Vignettes / Daniel Soha.

Names: Soha, Daniel, 1952- author.

Description: Short stories.

Identifiers: Canadiana (print) 20230158986 |
Canadiana (ebook) 20230159028 |

ISBN 9781771617000 (softcover) | ISBN 9781771617017 (PDF) |
ISBN 9781771617024 (EPUB) | ISBN 9781771617031 (Kindle)

Classification: LCC PS8637.O32 V54 2023 | DDC C813/.6—dc23

Published by Mosaic Press, Oakville, Ontario, Canada, 2023.

MOSAIC PRESS, Publishers
www.Mosaic-Press.com
Copyright © Daniel Soha 2023

Printed and bound in Canada.

MOSAIC PRESS
1252 Speers Road, Units 1 & 2, Oakville, Ontario, L6L 5N9
(905) 825-2130 • info@mosaic-press.com • www.mosaic-press.com

To Thomas Scott
The Poet

About the Author

Born in Aix-en-Provence to Hungarian-speaking parents, Daniel Soha lived and studied in France until his mid-20s. He is the holder of a Masters of Education and a Master's Degree in Anglo-American studies from the University of Aix-Marseille. As part of his studies, he spent a year in the North of England, where he developed a love of English culture and dialects.

After graduating with a double Master's degree, what he calls "a series of fortunate events" caused him to embark on an international career as a diplomat, a director of cultural organizations and a translator, and he worked successively for the Alliance Française, the French government, the Toronto French School, the French Library and Cultural Center (Boston), the United Nations, and Morningstar – a leading financial research company. Over a 20-year span, he lived in New York, Paris, Singapore, Boston and Toronto, where he is still residing.

Apart from numerous articles, editorials, book reviews, and even cooking recipes and a comic strip, his most notable writings include five novels, one book of short stories, one book of editorial pieces, and the French translations of two poetry books by Oakville poet Thomas Scott.

He is a two-time finalist of the Trillium Book Prize, for his novels *La Maison* (2009) and *Le Manuscrit* (2012). He also won on two occasions the Christine-Dumitriu-Van-Saanen prize, awarded by the French Book Fair in Toronto, for his novels *L'Orchidiable* (2009) and *Chroniques Tziganes II* (2018).

In 2015, he was selected to be one of the participants of the landmark literary project *Les 24 Heures du Roman*, where 24 renowned francophone authors got together on a 24-hour train ride from Moncton to Toronto and wrote 24 chapters of a novel (published under the name "*Sur les Traces de Champlain*") to celebrate the 400th anniversary of Samuel de Champlain's discovery of Upper Canada.

Vignettes, a collection of short stories, is Daniel Soha's first book written in the English language.

Published Works

Chroniques tziganes (fiction – Éditions du GREF, Toronto, 2004)

Amour à mort (fiction – GREF, Toronto, 2005)

User's Guide to a Blank Wall/Mode d'emploi pour un mur vide (translations of poems by Thomas Scott – GREF, Toronto, 2006).- Winner: Discovery Night at the Toronto Art Bar

Du Cœur au Ventre (a collection of articles and other editorial pieces – GREF, Toronto, 2007)

La Maison (fiction – GREF, Toronto, 2009) – Finalist: Trillium Book Award

L'Orchidiable (fiction– GREF, Toronto, 2009) – Winner: CDVS Prize

How Things Got Like This/Comment on en est arrivé là (translations of poems by Thomas Scott – GREF, Toronto, 2010)

Le Manuscrit (fiction – GREF, Toronto 2012) – Finalist: Trillium Book Award

Chroniques tziganes II (fiction – GREF, Toronto, 2018) – Winner: CDVS Prize

Table of Contents

Foreword

There are two questions that a writer does not like to hear. The first one is: "How did you become a writer?"

A trick question, in my view, based on a presupposition presented as fact. Actually, you do not *become* a writer. You *are* one, like you may be a sweetheart or a sourpuss, short, tall, handsome or double-jointed.

There is a wonderfully dismissive expression in English which, although not providing a smidgeon of an explanation or information we do not already know, offers in rather marvelous fashion a self-sufficient deflection:

"That's what I do."

Almost as satisfactory as "It is what it is".

Incidentally, French writer Hubert Monteilhet, in the penultimate story of this book, gives his own derisive, desacralizing, disrespectful answer, which I find most... apropos.

Look it up.

The other question is: "What is your book about?"

Although I have had many chances to explore how to express my irritation, from jocular to matter-of-fact and from unfazed to expansive, my general message always revolved around the same themes – my general irritation with people and humanity! For decades I have lived in English-speaking countries and most of my friends and my colleagues have been anglophones. So why express this general irritation to a minority when I can do so to the majority – this time in English rather than French.

Being also a translator, my first idea for a better reach was to translate my own work.

Wrong move.

I learned the hard way what has been drilled into the mind of every self-respecting translator: you always translate *into* you own native language, and not the other way around – and for those who are hesitant about what their first language is, it is quite simply the language you spontaneously count in. Having painstakingly tried to mold the English language around a French short story I wrote and which I thought must be made accessible to humanity at large as a matter of public interest, I asked the opinions of the people I thought were the closest to absolute bilingualism: my daughters.

It is only after weeks of nagging that I got a somewhat embarrassed answer:

"Well papa, it's well-written, grammatically correct and sometimes even with a rather rich vocabulary. There is only one problem…"

"Oh?"

"Nobody would speak like that."

Ouch.

Back to the drawing board. But I was stubborn and vain. I tried another story. Same verdict. Then another, and the best response I got was: "it's a great story but it sounds like a few things could be rephrased. Let me look into it."

Eventually, those three or four stories took months of rewriting by a small army of family and friends before they could take on any sort of English existence, and even so, they were not real translations, they had to be *adapted*, as it was not so much about expressing reality differently anymore, as expressing a different reality. And in the process, I realized that there are many brands of English: British and North American, of course, but also slang (many different iterations of it), medical or legalese, for instance. My specialty was *Translational*. A case in point: the length of my English translations was very close to that of the original French texts, which strongly suggests that my English was not *impressionistic*, which it should have been, but... *"explanational"*. I thus became a learned graduate of translational English, with an explanational minor.

In short, I had to resign myself to a rather glum conclusion: if I occasionally soar to certain heights with the shimmering elegance of a bird of paradise in French, my English translations fly with the gracefulness of a turkey.

Depressing.

But then something happened.

An idea.

What if instead of trying to translate my French stories I decided to write new ones directly in English? Maybe then I would bypass my obsessional urge to inflict the cookie cutter treatment to the English language, and freely make new cookies instead, with whatever basic ingredients I could find. After all, Samuel Beckett wrote directly in French to clear his mind of clutter and avoid the agony of too many choices. Maybe it will help me rediscover core values, like candor and simplicity.

And humility.

Maybe also I will have the satisfaction to convince the reader, with due reverence this time, that the answer to both questions of how I became a writer and what my books are about, like the proof of the pudding, is in the eating.

And these 'cookies' are the very best I could make.

Birchmount

My rosemary bush is thirsty. I see it right there, sitting on my Scarborough cliff, all bent over and looking despondent among the birch trees in the damp summer heat. I am attempting to bring variety to this thick, solid-green Northern landscape by colonizing it with Mediterranean plants from back home. I take my watering can, empty it thoroughly at the base of my rosemary, which instantly rewards me with a grateful whiff: long, heady, intense.

For a few seconds, the veil is torn; through the tear, plethoric sensations from another world, another time, gush in. My eyes become multifaceted like a bee's, able to look everywhere at once, and ripples of colour sweep over my chameleon's body. I hear the deafening noise of cicadas in the pines, I smell the sap. I feel the heat, its dusty waves entrapped in the red rocks of the Estérel hills. I feel the warm caress of an antique sea on my skin, and the strokes of a fragrant wind, cooling me off and making me hungry. My visions are suddenly populated by oleander and tamarisk, by the magical light and luxuriant tones from which emerged Matisse, Cézanne, Van Gogh… I wonder what sense of belonging Ulysses and Moses had, whether they felt they were part of a coherent world governed by continuity, unity, eternity, or were they just vested, at the dawn of humanity, with the exhausting and lonely task of giving it meaning and substance?

Ironically, it is the continuity inherited from their ancient world I have turned away from. Once again, I sense that my frequent, thunderous rejection of it is only a dogged, futile effort to make my exile bearable. I think of Ulysses and his twenty years of vagrancy. I think of Moses and his forty years of desert. I think of the myth of the Promised Land. I know that living "*elsewhere*" requires forgetting everything that once was, the same way breaking away from the women we once loved requires hating them with all our might, burning them with their letters and their pictures. In order to live on, we must betray. I know. It is the price to pay for numbing our emotions and our pain.

But already, little by little, the tear is mending itself, the wound self-cauterizes. My rosemary — uneventful, unambiguous, universal — calmly looks at me here the same way it did in the hills of my childhood home. Soon, I am only left with the sugary scent of freshly cut grass, the fragrance of my daily life: a Northern smell, a reassuring smell, a smell I have learned to embrace.

An English smell.

Family Tree

In the old days, the South of France was not France... not yet, or not entirely. It even spoke a different language – a *patois*, they called it, but it was decidedly not French. They made it French by setting fire to its pine groves and condominionizing it, by siccing on it wave after wave of wealthy old fogies and alien settlers, they made it French by turning it into Florida, by repopulating it, depersonalizing it, folklorizing it. They made it French by americanizing it.

One day, with a paltry sum he wanted to invest, my father staked his claim: he bought a plot of land with a little labourer's cabin buried in vines. There was an abundance of grapes, but also olives, almonds and two twin trees that produced totally identical apricots. Only when you tasted them did you notice that the fruit of the first one were very sweet but dry and the other's were dripping with an exquisite liquor, and you would marvel that desserts and jam were growing on trees.

At the very back of the vineyard, near a well set in a towering bush of laurels, there was a cherry tree with fruit so good that I thought in my childhood they were surely the famed manna of the Bible. Of the three cherry trees on the property, it was the most remarkable by far. The most experienced farmers, the most learned botanists scratched their heads under its branches wondering what kind of cherries they were. And Mr. Moustier, who lived further down in the valley, still remembered its fruit, which he was pilfering in his early childhood. Mr. Moustier was ninety-five years old.

The fruit of "the tree from the well" were rather large but unremarkable-looking, of a lighter, less appetizing red than the cherries you could find in the markets. The crop was small, the yield more than mediocre. They were unsellable, unmarketable, unexploitable even if you wanted to, the whole thing was an anachronism, an absurdity doomed to extinction. My father did everything he could to save the tree: he poured cement in its ant-ridden trunk, tied it with iron wire, cleaned it, deloused it, sprayed it, protected it with straw, trimmed it with tender care, and we all sang songs under its shriveled leaves. It is with utter horror that we followed its hopeless decline over a twenty-year span. The last year, it was by a pure miracle, a mysterious wave of life still radiating through shreds of bark, that the tree was able to produce a handful of delights.

Then, my father came up with the idea of grafting its last branches on the wild regrowths of another cherry tree. He did a dozen of those grafts, which died out, one after the other, as though the kindness he was trying to force upon sterile brambles had a poisonous effect on them, as though nature had suddenly turned mean.

The cherry tree from the well nevertheless performed its last miracle by fertilizing a single one of those grafts, and we waited for its fruit with great impatience. It was different, unique also, but no longer the taste of my childhood.

The cherry tree from the well died the year after the grafts. So did my father.

A Forgettable Man

He was a man of little consequence. A factory worker, married to a schoolteacher, had two kids, a son and a daughter. He spoke very little, kept to himself.

From the time he retired, he only wore his blue overalls, except to go to weddings, funerals and festive events. He did not even attend church: he was a socialist, and that was not in his DNA. He let his wife go and pray for his soul, but she did not find it very useful because he was a good man and there was no need to go to such extremes, so she occasionally gave him a tender thought and perfunctorily said the Lord's Prayer once more than confession required.

He pretty much stayed in his garage all the time, fiddling around with motors and mechanisms of all kinds, fixing hair dryers or vacuum cleaners, making shelves or re-varnishing old furniture: there is always something that needs fixing in a house, always more shelves to be cut.

When he first forgot where he had put his keys, nobody paid much attention: there were duplicates all around the house, and his slightly moody reaction went largely unnoticed. They found the keys later in the fridge where the beers were kept, and it triggered a good laugh. He even joined in.

Then he started forgetting words. It was not very important because words were not his *forte*, so whoever he was talking to would just fill in the blanks. But in any case he was not talking very much, so that was not much of a disturbance.

He had developed a ritual: on Sundays, when his wife was at church, his son would come and they had a game of dominoes. He visibly relished the exercise: his face would light up and they would compete fiercely, exchanging laconic remarks on strategy and bantering outrageously with bombastic words, the way simple people do. They never said anything about the fun they had with each other, their mutual appreciation: the dominoes said it all, because if the father and the son did not love each other, there would be no dominoes, and the working-class culture was one of deeds, not overinflated, useless statements.

Most times, he would win, because he was good.

When he started forgetting how to fix things, everybody realized that maybe he had a "condition". It was no easy feat to take him to a doctor and get diagnosed, but he eventually obliged, and the diagnosis was exactly what had been expected and dreaded. He did not react to the news: he was in one of his dark moods, so he just went to the garage and set up the board for a game of dominoes with his son. The next Sunday, they got together, they played and they had a good time. They even spoke a little.

As months went by, he forgot everything: the names of his relatives and friends, the story of his life, how to go to the hardware store, how to drive his car, and eventually he even forgot himself. Did he realize it? Probably, one way or another, because his mood got darker. The only reprieve he got from his condition was on Sundays: miraculously, by a shred of intuition, he still knew when his son would come, he would set up the board an hour ahead of time and wait, doing nothing. When his son came in, he would brighten up and they played.

He had long forgotten how to speak, but there was a twinkle in his eye and he was still a fierce opponent.

One Sunday, when his son came, he was late in setting the board and had to be helped. The game started, laboriously, and it soon became evident that he would no longer be able to play, that the rules of the game were gone to oblivion too. With unspeakable cruelty, nature inflicted one last horror on him: awareness. From the bottom of his mental abyss, he must have known, because he suddenly stood up, and in a fit of rage, he trashed the board and abruptly left.

That same night, he forgot how to breathe.

Boulevard Diderot

My old friend Maurice had rented us a little apartment he owned in the 13th district of Paris, across the street from the army barracks. In true French style, the appliances were clunky relics, and the paint job was left to the tenants – us. Juli had never seen such a slum, such a shabby kitchen, such grungy walls; she suddenly got into a slump, I had to be extra considerate to surround our decaying lifestyle with a semblance of romanticism.

But still, it was on the 9th floor, with a view of sorts, and a little outdoor terrace. The elevator only went up to the seventh because two extra floors had been added on years after the main construction was completed, and we had to wind through a series of narrow, steep, dark hallways to get eventually to our hovel in the sky. As the thought of bringing up our oversized designer furniture through that steep and narrow maze was preposterous, we had no other recourse than to hire at great expense one of the three hydraulic cranes that existed in the whole city of Paris, and pray that our furniture could somehow be pushed in through the windows.

Our quest for a low-profile, peaceful life got off to a bad start, when the arrival of this equipment caused a crowd to gather on the sidewalk, hordes of people with their noses in the air, speculating on the cause of commotion.

"I'm telling you it's a cat that got stuck on the roof!"

"Absolutely not!... It's somebody who's trying to commit suicide, I saw that sort of thing before on TV!"

Eventually, even the superintendent of the building, a large woman with a particularly hideous overbite, and her alcoholic son who was pacing the sidewalk in his fuzzy slippers, appeared uncertain and even joined in the gossip: although duly notified of our intent they suddenly seemed shaken by the authoritativeness of some of those statements and no longer knew what to think. Only when the first couch rose up in the air did the crowd let out a droning "aaaaaaaaah!" of understanding and relief.

It is on that day that I first met our eighth-floor neighbour, a dignified and reserved old gentleman whom I got into the habit of saluting in the hallways. This act of recognition, at once polite and good-humoured, grew out of the contrast between his formality and our repeated instances of physical intimacy as we often shared the tiny, rickety Parisian elevator where full body contact was unavoidable. After a few rides it became necessary to ease the discomfort of a casual or surprise encounter with a friendly word or gesture.

A couple of months after meeting the old gentleman, I was walking down the two floors to get to the elevator and saw its door closing. I made a mad dash and managed to stick my arm inside, and the door slid open. I found myself face to face with the old fellow, decked out in a dark, three-piece suit. I saluted him as usual, but for the first time he did not acknowledge me, his eyes seemingly lost in private thoughts. Next to him was another gentleman who frantically gestured me to move away. No problem, there's no room, I'll walk down.

When I got to the main floor I saw my neighbour again, snugly resting in a wooden box lined with pink satin.

Obviously embarrassed, the building superintendent dragged me by the sleeve to a corner of the lobby to whisper an explanation.

Mr. Laporte had passed away in his apartment a couple of days earlier. The staircase and the elevator were both too tight for the coffin, so they waited for *rigor mortis* to set in to stand the body up one last time in the elevator and sneak it downstairs. In order for the old gentleman's body to remain inconspicuous in any chance encounter with unsuspecting bystanders, his eyes were left open.

"You understand, sir, it's not exactly legal to go around public spaces with a stiff in tow, so I could not let you know, but I very much count on your utmost discretion."

"Naturally, Madam, I understand perfectly... But tell me, who was that other person in the elevator?"

"Well, the guy from the funeral parlour... *naturellement.*"

Welcome to Paris.

All Love Stories Are Failures,
Except the One We Are Currently Living

I nearly grew old.
Just like that – I didn't pay attention.
Too close to call.

It was Laurette who prevented me. She strictly forbade it.

She refused to see me as a castaway or even consider it as an option. She blew my sail, firmly grabbed my rudder, straightened out my mast, and sternly lay across my big bad bow. She puffed and she blew, sloshed around in my internal sewer and flushed me through the gills, brought me back to life, and I grew addicted to her mouth-to-mouth resuscitation. A mermaid run aground for my sake, she was banished to thick air, and I wined her in celebration.

I emerged.

Laurette is a 90-pound categorical imperative, with eyes like fjords exquisitely drowning her whole face, then radiating their intensity around, absorbing the dullest of landscapes or fragmenting it into prisms and luminous mirrors, bathing its most innocuous objects in greyish-blue hues and making them as precious as aquamarines: devouring, bulimic eyes whose voracity I craved, desperately hoping that their cannibalistic workings would make them my last resting place. Once you have seen this miracle, my friend, once you have taken possession of that beauty, it becomes the only filter giving you a coherent, permanent and acceptable vision of the world, and there is no way you can still look at the murky puddle of everyday life, however sacramentally blessed it might have been, and find in it the crystalline virtues of spring water.

****

She enters the room, tiny and illuminated by her own radiance, and day breaks out, silence descends, souls hum celestial melodies, a pregnant pause sets in. One day, that Aphrodite had frivolously decided to come down among us mortals, probably for lack of purpose, because it is said that the Gods get very bored with their eternal mission of just being there, and just for believers. She found herself a fallen angel's occupation as a waitress in a greasy spoon where people ate hamburgers and listened to rockabilly. I would go there every day at opening time, I couldn't help myself, and watch her flutter from one table to another, her bust tightly strapped in a black blouse that gave her face the crisp radiance of a summer morning, her feet in modest Cinderella's ballet slippers from which emerged ankles of a slightly milky, aristocratic flesh imploring the desperate peeping Tom that I was to uncover them, paw them, discover their rosy tints, disconcert them, debauch them before I would randomly uncover another part of her mystery. My nose in my beer, I watched the noses of the other customers, also in their beer, and savoured with rapture the injustice of which I was the inexplicable, unfair beneficiary, because even though I couldn't pierce the mystery, I was at least invited to penetrate it regularly, with a dart overwhelmed by its own power but diligent and love-crazed.

To be tolerable, beauty must be moral and virtuous, in other words it must make itself available: sell itself or offer itself. Although Laurette had offered it to me, I had insisted at that moment on giving her a modest sum, a kind of subsidy, or rather an offering that suited the liturgical character of our relationship, because without it I wouldn't have considered myself worthy to receive her, and only saying a word would have damned me. We thus had a unique and respectable arrangement by which the fifty-something-year-old that I was hopefully avoided ridicule by competing in the realm of husbands, fiancés, boyfriends or other possible lovers of this young girl, without being stuck with the vulgar label of sugar-daddy. In my field I would be the best, and even, with a bit of luck, the only one, and I could then aspire to a total and exclusive love.

And I received and still receive a total and exclusive love.

That kind of love at least.

****

As pitiful as I may sound, there is one strength I recognize I had: I dared give in to my weaknesses, capitulate before everything that was beautiful or pleasant, had the immense strength of character to throw myself deliberately at pleasure when I knew perfectly well, like everyone does, that it was immoral and that it led nowhere. For everything else, work, family, country, I stalled, I calmed things down, I pulled the wool over people's eyes, I limited the damage. But I nevertheless gave life and it still overjoys me.

So it happened just like that. With coherence and determination and in all the proud, dauntless legitimacy of my free will I surrendered to Laurette, to her obvious superiority, her devastating beauty. And then, I who thought once again that this would be a dead end, I have been rewarded for this honesty, this courage and this lucidity, I have reaped the dividends and the interest, even though I didn't even know that it was an investment and I certainly didn't have the soul of a stockbroker. And besides, who's counting?

Suddenly, I was forbidden to grow old.

On pain of death.

GPS

Victor turned on his GPS, even though he knew the way. He had gotten into the habit of competing with the Virtual Lady ever since he started suspecting that she was not infallible – just craved to "show" his inventiveness about the alternate routes he would choose, and maybe shut up that smug, impassible, disembodied voice. Real artificial intelligence, he thought, would have the Creature stammer and fumble, then maybe apologize. Artificial intelligence would have to invent artificial stupidity.

"Head North", she had told him once, as he was trying to find his way through a maze of warehouses by the airport in the middle of a storm. "How am I supposed to know where the North is? Do I have a compass?"

And why a female voice? Why a North American accent? Real artificial intelligence, he thought, would hijack the voice of his gas station attendant: a 70-year-old former rickshaw driver from Mumbai. At least, it would be an alternate truth, if not a better reflection of it.

And why was it a lady instructing him where to go? In his whole life, he had never met a female who had a sense of direction or distances, never mind a spatial perspective – no male chauvinism intended.

Or maybe he just turned on the GPS for company.

15

DANIEL SOHA

His daughter Claire always said he drove like an old man – even before he became one. His answer was always the same: "I *am* an old man!" It was just a game they played, or maybe a sign of reconnaissance, a reassuring code: "I am here, you are here, we are still the same, thank God!" It was a bit irritating, still.

He had dropped Claire off at her home before driving on. She was in a very picky mood, nagged him about the way he was cutting the curves of highway ramps by encroaching on the white lines delineating what was intended to be the shoulder. Between the Virtual Lady and the Virtuous Daughter, there was no way out. Thankfully, Claire's intelligence was not artificial.

He had tried to explain that cutting the curves gave a vehicle more stability, that instead of slowing down in the middle of the curve he could even accelerate, that it made adherence to the asphalt better. She understood perfectly, but found his remark irrelevant: this was not a Formula One race, and since he was old already, the least he could do was abide by the rules of the road.

Oh? Was that unlawful?

After he dropped her off, he decided against driving on the highway: too boring, and maybe he would spot an attractive store window in Suburbia on this lethal Sunday: an unexpected oasis of curios in an ocean of predictability, like a Mauritian grocer selling a genetically engineered clone of the extinct dodo bird. That would be something, 'eh?

Such were the vagrancies of his wandering mind.

It started to rain, and the car was running out of fuel. He welcomed the entertaining thought of stopping at a gas station and picking up a bag of Ruffles and a Diet Coke, then hitting the road again and turning on the CBC, hardly audible for now, but whose reception he knew would be better in a few kilometers.

16

Everything went according to plan: the gas, the Diet Coke, the Ruffles, and he even picked up one of those beef sausage sticks, the long, spicy kind, with a list of ingredients only a product made in the USA would dare to display. No dodo bird, but it would have to do.

"On the road again" – a tune he inescapably hummed ever since it came out in the 60s, each time he would go on a trip. Alan "Blind Owl" Wilson, of the 27 Club, from a time when poet Jim Morrison decreed that no great man was to reach 30. Victor was 72, a sort of anachronic anagram. No liquor, no drugs, not even tobacco. Just a lingering yearning, the memory of a memory.

Seat belt.
Yes Ma'am
Was that the GPS?

At the last second, Victor changed his mind. Maybe he wanted to get home faster, and maybe he just wanted to outpace, out-manoeuvre the GPS, see what would happen. He took the highway.

It all worked out perfectly: the ramp, the encroaching, the acceleration. It is only when he reached the feeder lane that the vehicle aquaplaned.

****

Victor looked around and found the situation vaguely funny. The steering wheel was split in half and had gotten out of reach, and a pathetic, laughable blimp seemed to have taken possession of his living space. He found the position of his body a little strange, but didn't give it a second thought. Outside, the world had capsized and the white line on the road was the only thing he could see in his window. "The white line? But I cleared it!", he thought. Was it another white line? After all, it really didn't matter. He felt a little dizzy, a little numb. Nothing to write home about. For a second, he thought he might want to open the door – that's what you're supposed to do after a car crash, isn't it? He almost tried to reach the handle, noticed the broken glass and decided against it. It could wait. Right now, he was too sleepy: not surprising, the trip was so boring! Maybe he could just have a nap for a few minutes, wait till they cleaned the broken glass, and then he would again go all gung-ho, his usual uplifting self, perhaps apologize for the disturbance and help them clean up the mess. He smiled at the thought.

Just before he closed his eyes and the fire broke out, he heard a voice, clear as a bell – a female voice:

"Continue on highway 401 for 17 kilometers".

Gelato

I had decided to kill myself.
I had everything prepared, nothing was left to chance.

My house had been sold, my last will drawn up, my clothes folded into neat little piles and donated to a charity, my furniture had all but gone to the flea market, and for my last night I had booked a room in the most luxurious hotel in town, where I planned to loot the minibar and run up a tab that I would never settle since I had gone out of my way, in the nick of time, to cancel my credit cards. I had also decided to resist the temptation of a last act of solitary pleasure, dreading the mental and moral void that would have resulted from that hopeless titillation. No, I wanted to leave replete but still with the memory of an appetite, a dash of libido; I wanted to leave as an aesthete, an artist, a philosopher.

I was happy: my children would lack for nothing, neither would the no-less than adorable creature who had driven me to this act of despair, and there were only those few coins I had kept in my pocket just in case which still needed to be spent. I would wait until the last moment for that.

The day of my ultimate, irreparable gesture, I had a hearty breakfast at the hotel: bacon cooked just right, with the rind still strong but lined with a layer of slightly quivering fat which toned down its saltiness; small English breakfast sausages rancid to perfection, and three servings of slightly runny scrambled eggs; a freshly squeezed orange juice with lots of pulp; an American coffee with a dash of real milk – a beverage that I loved with this type of buffet but that I snobbishly poo-pah'ed every time I had company, toasted multi-grain bread that I had buttered while dutifully and lovingly producing the usual characteristic scratching sound with my knife, and that I had covered with a thin layer of orange marmalade - in a nutshell: a delight.

With a peaceful, yet wandering mind, I grabbed a newspaper which I devoured with equally great avidity, regretting all the same that I didn't have to pay for it because it would have enabled me to dispose of those few coins that distorted my pockets and made a little metallic friction sound, like a bunch of keys, when I walked.

I had always said, to whomever would listen, that the day I died, one of my last acts would be to get a shoeshine. The time had come to see if it would give me the satisfaction I expected. Having thought about it too much, I only experienced moderate pleasure, too brief and insufficiently intense.

I had one last thing to do, for good measure.

I had always been a great lover of ice cream and chocolate, so it made sense that I should end my life a prey to this lavish taste and this sneaky enzyme which allegedly emulates the emotion of love, further empowered by emulsions of champagne on Valentine's Day.

Two blocks away was an Italian ice cream parlour serving particularly exquisite dark chocolate gelati, and, what's more, on a waffle cone. It was perfectly timely, it would all come full circle: all calculations done, with a measured but gracious tip, I would use up my last penny.

So it was both with a feeling of purpose and fulfillment that I put my last coin in the little jar on the counter and dutifully began to smear my face with dark chocolate.

I hadn't gone thirty feet before I suddenly had, on the verge of death, the vision that changed my life.

A derelict creature, homeless and filthy, was pacing the sidewalk, begging loudly for the alms that would allow him to live another day, with heartbreaking sincerity and drama. He was a relatively young man still, grungy and with the orangey complexion of alcoholics, who showed positively no sign that he would ever come out of the hole. I suddenly felt for him in deep, meaningful fashion, I even cried, and I was not born yesterday: I am perfectly trained to spot those impostors who lead a relatively dignified and clean life and who only abuse the compassion of passers-by to secure a few extra pints of beer – windshield washers, aggressive beggars who are later seen in some tavern laughing at the good trick they played.

I have an infallible criterion of judgment: the feet. I always look at a panhandler's feet. Many of those people, especially when they sleep on the sidewalks, have very clean feet, with trimmed nails; this suggests, if not a sham, at least regular visits to well-outfitted shelters which, all things considered, are guarantors of a minimal dignity of life. But if I see feet wrapped in dirty bandages, sticking through filthy socks, or swollen, purplish and almost unbearable to watch, the reality of the misfortune that strikes those people is obvious to me.

The misfortune that had struck this young man indeed seemed real, for his feet were beyond repulsive. I belched an instant sob into my freshly-shaved jowls.

"… to eat, I beg you!..." Something to eat !!!!"

I rummaged through my pocket. Not the slightest forgotten coin, no small bill that passed through the dryer, crimped and half-bleached. I wasn't going to give him my freshly polished shoes: it would not be in keeping with the decorum of this act of compassion.

"Something to eat! Something to eat!...", he bawled in heart-rending howls.

It was then that the only magnanimous and plausible idea occurred to me – an initiative which, moreover, would bring me overwhelming gratitude and place me in the good graces of the Lord at the point of death: a colossal sacrifice made in a last ripple of life, for the sake of preserving another man's, or at least of making it more bearable.

I offered him my triple gelato, with only one mouthful missing.

The bastard threw it in my face and called me an asshole.

The Wink

B efore every one of his outrageous statements, Jack would always assume a pensive air, and then, his lips hinting a shadow of a smile, wink at me with a sarcastic twinkle. They say that this is what actors do to fend off stage fright, symbolically addressing a single member of the audience and forgetting all others in their focus. Oh, I know, the gaze may have been like the eerie eyes of those portraits that seem to follow you wherever you go. Chances are that everyone listening to him felt the same intense attention, but I cherished the belief that he was playing to me, and only to me.

And play it was, certainly hard and judgmental at times, yet impish and theatrical. Those were dark times in our country, and you could not speak your mind, especially in public. Seemingly oblivious of such restrictions, Jack thundered against the regime, allegorically stormed the Almighty Party with clever and unparalleled verbal violence, restoring to us a memory of innocence and facetiousness. We flocked to him as often as we could, before his game would evanesce into reality or unreality. We knew that this could not possibly last.

Since public meetings were forbidden, Jack picked the university as his forum. After registering for an obscure philosophy course, first he diligently subverted it through sheer strength of intellect and thirst for freedom. Then he simply took possession of it, the professor becoming hardly more than a ghostly foil to his power. The bureaucracy was slow to react. Minor offences were summarily and expeditiously punished, but the lumbering regime was ill-equipped to fight real, open and deliberate acts of rebellion: it needed time to rally its antibodies. Or maybe, we thought, the State wanted to give us the illusion of freedom, having convinced itself through its own propaganda that the average citizen, after decades of dictatorship, had had enough indoctrination, and that the "Jack phenomenon" would die a natural death in the face of general apathy.

What happened was precisely the opposite. Little by little, Jack's audience grew, coming to his class as if it were a popular performance, eagerly listening to this immensely talented orator rage against the false truths that this washed-out propaganda machine was still attempting to force onto us. People were flabbergasted that such an anachronous voice still existed. You didn't even have to agree with him, sedition simply meant being there, letting yourself get tainted by its corrosive grin. Lecture by lecture, Jack became the talk of the campus. He became untouchable, even mythical: there was nothing he could not do. Even at his age, he could have swept all the girls off their feet, with his beautiful grayish mane and his exquisitely weathered face, its furrows chiseled by mysterious battles. But he was not interested in that, I could tell from the ironic quality of his smile, from his caustic winks.

The lack of any reaction from the system helped to imbue Jack with an aura of invincibility. He was thought to be invulnerable. Some even believed that the regime was powerless to respond, that it was in an irreversibly decadent downspin, finished, and bound for a collapse.

As for me, I said little. I was afraid to expose myself because I simply could not dispel the possibility that our improbable

Jack was a provocateur planted to spot potential dissidents and nip their insidious ideas in the bud. Secretly though, I sincerely hoped that Jack was the initiator of something genuine and powerful, reviving with his flamboyance the spark in us all. No oppression could extinguish such sparks. I caught myself believing in human nature again.

Jack's fall was that much more painful. When they finally came to get him, he said nothing. There were no diatribes, nor swearing, nor any grandstanding for a change. He smiled a little, slightly shrugged his shoulders, finished his coffee, picked up his jacket and left, flanked by two bodyguards. He ambled at a steady and calm pace, as though he was going to the supermarket or the movies.

Appearing out of nowhere, a priggish, ivy-league type explained to us that Jack was known to be seriously ill. Despite a severe chemical imbalance in his brain, he obstinately refused to take his medication, but the matter was now under control and he would return as soon as his treatment was finished. The preppie was called a bastard and a son of a bitch and the like, and everybody ganged up on him, coming so close to beating him that he had to retreat amidst a hail of boos and hisses. Depression then fell on us like a block of lead and flattened us for months.

Jack came back the next semester. People swarmed to greet him, shake his hand and congratulate him. They patted him on the back, but in the midst of all this outpouring of affection everyone could sense that he was different, that his unique smile had changed. He went to sit at his usual spot like a regular student, still brighter than most, his intelligence belied by that new dull look in his eyes, that frequent stare into the distance, that fixedness, that unfamiliar sullenness. This "normality" was the *coup de grâce* for us, even more so than his arrest. I think that we reached bottom right there and then, as we recognized our own impotence. At that moment we *knew* that the system had won decisively. Its stroke of genius was to give us back a Jack who had been normalized, conditioned, integrated, homogenized. It was to infuse us with the certainty and inevitability of defeat.

How dangerous and perhaps futile it is to play with Nature's determinism. All the sorcerers' apprentices and all the Frankensteins of this world are never entirely the masters of what they aspire to create, and perhaps this is where the tiny window of hope lies. One day, right in the middle of a presentation of Kant's categories, Jack inexplicably and suddenly broke out into laughter. It was a clear and candid laugh, as though he had just heard a really good joke. This irrationality, this apparent madness chilled us to the bone. Most of us managed to keep our composure, some even laughed with him, albeit ever so faintly.

A few seconds later, I stole a furtive glance at Jack, terrified that I would read in his eyes an insanity such that I could not bear. His eyes still stared into some unknown distance, but I saw in them an intensity I thought I recognized, something warmly familiar. My heart leaped. Suddenly departing from his distant search, Jack seemed to wake up as though shaking off a dream. Slowly he surveyed the auditorium, and even though I was quite far, I was sure that he spotted me. Then, I swear he smiled faintly.

… and yes, he winked at me.

Translator, Traitor

I open the freezer, grab the bottle, take another slug. The gin sends its icy flow down my throat, and into a vine-like network of channels in my chest that I wouldn't otherwise know exist.

I've gotten into the habit of keeping my gin in the freezer because of the profound dissatisfaction of using ice for my dry Martinis, whether straight up or on the rocks: I'd like to fancy myself as a kind of James Bond figure authoritatively enforcing the "stirred, not shaken" imperative, but my cocktails always end up watered down or not cold enough, and if all those years of drinking have taught me something, it is that the potency of the basic commodity has to be given full justice. No frills. So, since the petroleum flavour of gin must be preserved, I freeze it. Purity is at stake.

And as a bonus, I get an oily substance, quite pleasant to the eye, almost like mercury or molten lead.

It is 7 AM.

I got the phone call around 5 PM yesterday, but only responded two hours later.

The Ambassador again, on my private line, probably getting blue in the face over the urgency of making me genuflect at one of his obsessions. They even got me a red phone, like in the Kremlin.

I let it ring.

I never respond instantly, just because.

This is Singapore, I am running an "arm's length" organization for the French government. I want to stretch that arm to the limit, and he's trying to twist it.

Technically, the Ambassador is not my boss, but he still lays claim to the little power I have. My existence irritates him, he wants me to worship His Supreme Being, and in His eyes I am just a bottom-feeder.

It is an existential truth.

He is a mixture of Bela Lugosi and Al Pacino in "Devil's Advocate." Pasty white complexion, red eyes and a toothy snarl. I call him T-Rex.

He is terrifying.

I made an appointment at the French embassy for 8 PM. I thought this would give me a reprieve until today. But no, they reopened the embassy for me. What an honour! It was my punishment for not answering the phone.

T-Rex did not grace me with his presence either. Sent one of his spineless henchmen, visibly distraught at having to miss some of the lewd moistures of expat life, the desire-by-the-pool, chlorine-enhanced sex ritual.

"Sir, we'll have the visit of a French delegation tomorrow and His Excellency would like you to act as an interpreter – French to English and English to French."

I shrugged.

"I am not an interpreter."

"Our interpreter is indisposed and we can think of no better replacement."

Does he think I'm flattered? They're just broke, they don't want to spend the money.

I refuse.

He mumbles something in his breath, unconvincingly but dutifully. I make out a few words, like "report", "uncooperative", "unfortunate", "career."

The alternative is to do it or get fired. Do or die, as usual.

I guess that in those spheres, being threatened is the closest you get to being begged.

I am dying for a Wild Turkey on the rocks.

I accept.

"Who are the members of the delegation?"

"The French Minister of Foreign Affairs and three members of his cabinet."

JEEEE-ZUSSS!!!!!

****

I tossed and turned all night, slept maybe a couple of hours in a sweaty delirium, wondering if an inaccurate translation could trigger the third world war.

The complex of the impostor: "I'm not suited for this job, this job is not for me, never was. I lied and cheated my way throughout, I'm no good, not even trained, sooner or later they will notice, they are *bound* to notice."

Should I have a third slug? There is more than a slug left in the bottle, maybe two or three, that's more than I usually drink to "take the edge off." What the hell, three is a charm.

This time, I feel a pleasant numbness in my limbs.

****

The appointment is for 9 AM, I am at the Singaporean foreign ministry at 8:15. The Minister's executive assistant is there already. She looks a little surprised, but you know, I live far, I didn't want to be delayed by a traffic jam or a fender-bender.

I live far... Singapore is 20 kilometers by 40!

She smiles at me: a sexy librarian's smile, but a notch above. A tad slutty, or is it just wishful thinking? I don't really care. The anxiety has started again, the familiar lump in my throat. I need to control it.

She ushers me into a plush waiting room. Maybe reading a magazine will take my mind away from the decisive influence I will have in the disintegration of Singaporean/French relations. I wish I could have another slug.

****

From a bottomless void, an ink well of nothingness, I hear a faint cough, then a shy hello, then "the gentlemen are here." I open my eyes. She is in front of me, smiling almost affectionately. Definitely wishful thinking.

"You must be tired."

How did my mind, from the depths of its fog, conjure up the brilliant line I retorted?

"Not at all, I was meditating."

She is taken aback.

"You can disconnect just like that? Disappear into yourself? I meditate too, I've been trying for years. How do you do it?"

"It takes a lot of practice."

****

There are eight of us in the conference room: three Singaporeans including the Minister, then the French Minister of foreign affairs and three of his aides.

And the interpreter.

Me.

It starts off rather well. I am quite aware of the situation in Cambodia, so I can amble along. Not brilliantly, but decently. Not as tough as I thought. Should I try to keep an endearing smile, or will it look like a sneer? Or worse – the grin of an idiot? I choose to look professional, but put on a vaguely affected, "diplomatic" drawl. Nobody seems to notice.

Then they move on to economic exchanges. How dare they? Stay on topic, stay on topic, for God's sake!...

Aviation. Airlines. Should Air France have a stopover in Singapore?

What THE FUCK is a "right of first freedom"? I translate literally, without understanding anything, in a gust of hyperventilation. I stammer.

The third world war is minutes away.

Thank God, there's a coffee break. Should I make a break for it? Ask for a doctor? No way. I'm stuck. It's going to get worse. Sweat is pouring down my back, I hope it has not reached my armpits, but I don't dare to look. There's a drop on the tip of my nose. I try to wipe it off but I can only flick it into my eye. A burning sensation. Now I'm crying too.

One of the French guys is looking at me. He makes a welcoming gesture, invites me to get closer. A "nice guy" type of face. I am a little encouraged, but worried. I start to move in his direction, my legs feel like cotton wool.

"You look nervous."

No kidding.

"Well, don't be. We all speak perfect English. The reason we always ask for an interpreter is that the translation gives us a little bit of extra time to find the best diplomatic responses."

I'm suited for this job, this job is definitely for me.

Always was.

Mr. Rascal and Dr. Heid

" I am Dr. Heid", he said when I introduced myself. "How do you do."

"How do you do", I replied.

Being a rather knowledgeable fellow, I know that the proper response to "How do you do" is not "Fine, thanks!", or even "Very well, and yourself?", and certainly not something like "Swimmingly, but who's asking?", but... "how do you do." And no question mark please.

"How do you do" does not even rise to the level of a rhetorical question; it has emptied itself of any meaning and eradicated any form of intonation or expressiveness. In an absurd linguistic twist that only the British mind can entertain or even comprehend, the answer to "How do you do" is... "How do you do."

And to complete the emotional outpour one might derive from such a welcoming salutation, it has to come out as flat, toneless and mechanical as possible.

Unless it is just a ploy to humiliate Americans.

Hee haw.

There were three cultural institutions in Boston that swore allegiance to a foreign power. The Dante Alighieri Institute of our Italian friends was on the Cambridge side, near Harvard. I tried to meet my Italian colleague several times, but to no avail: either he could not make our appointment on time, or he cancelled at the last minute. One morning I simply decided to drop in on the odd chance I could catch him at the beginning of the working day. The building was open and empty, there was no-one in sight. Around 10:15, an Italian fellow with jet-black hair and striking blue eyes showed up, put on an apron with the logo of *La Pergola* printed in the front and offered to make me an espresso at the cafeteria while I was waiting. I gratefully accepted and we chatted for a few minutes, then I left.

It is only months later that I realized from a physical description made by a third party that my barista was probably the master of the house.

On the other side of the river, in the venerable Back Bay area, were the Goethe Institute and the French Cultural Centre. I was in charge of the latter, and Dr. Heid of the former.

The French, even though they seem to take the business of culture quite seriously, typically appoint to the leading role some adventurer who always seems to have usurped the position or gotten it as a reward for underhandedly defeating a scheming opponent. There is always a freebooter, pirate-like quality to us. And I'm not just talking about myself.

The Germans, conversely, pick their representatives out of a highly trained battalion of exquisitely refined individuals – all of them "Doctors", with an astonishing knowledge of the arts, philosophy, history, economics and many other disciplines that flatter the mind and enlighten it with humanistic fervour. Dr. Heid knew my music better than I did, my movies better than I did, and – irritatingly, my literature better than I did.

Before he introduced me to the visiting German Ambassador, a Von Hindenburg look-alike, he took me aside and whispered: "Don't mention the war. I did once but I think I got away with it", then burst into a noisy peal of laughter at my horrified expression. That was humour. A parody of John Cleese in "Fawlty Towers." The guy had his markers right.

Werner Heid was one of the very few people I ever found deeply, genuinely funny, in an almost burlesque kind of way. There was something profoundly hilarious emanating from his very persona; he must have known, because my constant giggles would otherwise have surely offended him. A tall, thin man whose rather stiff posture was belied by an obvious propensity to indulge in pleasures of the palate and the flesh, he embodied both Prussia and Bavaria and evoked an obsolete, conflicting clutter of spiked helmets, starched shirts, neck braces, swordsticks, clicking heels, ostrich feathers and monocles.

But the crowning achievement of his comic genius was the presence, in the front of his mouth, of a silver incisor that made every facetiousness glint, every smile glitter, every fit of expressive brilliance flash a sudden, awkward beam in the eyes of the beholder. I was stunned and mesmerized, like a deer in the headlights.

For a while, we would routinely have lunch, at least once or twice a month, at a sort of mock-Irish-chichi-upscale pub that could only exist in Boston. I was literally dazzled by the man, looking at him incredulously while he was talking in his haughty British accent where a hint of German parlance would only occasionally emerge when he was unfamiliar with the use of a word and the only speech he could produce was an oddly mispronounced version of it. Soon, one bottle of smoky Fetzer turned into two, and our meals ended in slurry banters. He made fun of my aversion to cheese, reprimanding me for being an embarrassment and a traitor to my own *kultur*, and I mocked "his" Anglo-Saxon world, where human communities consisted of ladies, gentlemen, in-betweens and doctors – a denomination transcending gender classifications in its obsessive pursuit of pomposity.

It is on a day of special elation, after the double sip of Bourbon with which I had washed down my bread pudding, that I decided to pick on him – I mean maybe a little more than I usually did.

"I love the way you handle the English language."

"Thank you."

"Very British, but in a good sense: you know, not like mine, which is more all-purpose, utilitarian if you will… more 'airport English', but with an accent… Your speech is clearly identifiable, culturally earmarked, distinguished without being snobbish, and it fits your role very well. A perfect match between the form and the substance."

"Really? That's nice to hear."

"There's only one suggestion I'd like to make, if I may."

"Oh?"

"Get rid of the stiffness. Americans are a rather relaxed bunch, very laid back, and they like informal introductions, which are more conducive to a friendly follow-up. The formality of a 'how do you do' is a dead-end, the negation of any further socializing unless you can seamlessly but acrobatically move on to an inexhaustible topic, like the weather… But it takes a British mind to do that, and we are not British…"

"I see… What do you propose?"

"I don't know, something more American, but please avoid 'How are you today?', because it suggests that you know the person and you are inquiring about their state of mind or their health, which must have been bad from the way the question is put… In addition, this is the typical telephone salutation of a telemarketer or someone who wants to sell you something, so keep off."

"What else?... 'How are you'?... 'Hello'? ... 'Hi'?..."

"Something more colloquial, more vernacular, with a local flavour..."

"Like?"

"Like... 'Howdy partner', maybe?"

"What does it mean?"

"Oh, it would be perfect! 'Howdy' is an abbreviation of 'How do you do'..."

"And why 'partner'?"

"Well, it's a term of endearment, sort of... You know how business-minded these people are, so calling someone a partner must have been a compliment originally... And it's hardly more than a figure of speech now, you know, like 'paying someone a visit': you don't really pay, do you...", or: 'paying tribute', or even 'paying attention' – in English, they make you pay for everything!..."

"Indeed..."

It was funny and we laughed.

Shortly thereafter, we each got more involved into the complexities of our own lives, and our lunch ritual was suspended. We called each other up quite often at first, then occasionally, then hardly at all, until we simply got afraid of running out of things to say at the realization that the Fetzer, previously an integral part of our chemistry, had no place in a telephone conversation.

One day, I got in the mail a fancy envelope with the familiar green logo. My heart leaped in my chest.

Werner.

I arrived at the October 3 reunification party as hundreds of guests were flocking in. In the distance, Werner was being the gracious host, kissing a lady's hand while she was giggling at something he told her. He saw me, waved effusively, and his smile flickered a familiar silvery spark into my eyes. He started heading my way.

Just before we connected, he was stopped in his tracks by some upper-class bejeweled matron, a typical groupie of his renowned chamber music series. Reaching for her hand to kiss, he clicked his heels, bowed politely, then uttered his *cri de cœur*:

"Howdy, baaadnah?"

Jacques

He was a big, burly man with a child's smile. His hands were like shovels, his complexion the colour of fresh ham, his flesh tenderized by Beaujolais. Behind his pipe and his glasses, a watchful eye could detect the humanity he was trying to conceal. He was a diplomat, and exterior signs of kindness in his field were indicative of a visible minority – tantamount to a death warrant.

In those days I was living in Asia, the allegedly independent director of a non-profit organization more or less subservient to the French government. My relationship with Jacques started off with a couple of formal one-on-ones, until I brought a bottle of Bordeaux to his office, claiming that since I was "invited", I couldn't possibly come empty-handed. We drank it together, made long, thoughtful pauses between sips, and once the bottle was finished he told me he preferred Burgundy.

Point well taken.

His latest posting had been in Beirut, where bombs were flying and French-speaking Arabic nuns and sundry dignitaries would return the subsidies that France, in her surrealistic wisdom, had given them to set up a library or sponsor some off-the-mark initiative, like the launching of a choir or the restoration of some relief dating back to ancient Maronite times. "Honestly, we do appreciate your generosity, but our convent is now a square block of rubble and ashes, God help us!" With a shaky hand, Mother Superior would dutifully write personal cheques to refund the persons to whom she attributed such gratuitous largesse.

To reward him for perpetuating government work in Armageddon, Jacques was given what was touted as a cushy job in Singapore. Never mind that he didn't speak a word of English, he spoke German and that was good enough. Just had to smooth out the stiffness and learn to pronounce a few words properly, like "gooberation." Never was he again to refer, under any circumstances, to "zusammenarbeit."

And speak German he did: the holder of a Ph.D. in Alemannic culture and languages and a former member of the French Communist Party, he had served as an interpreter to Erich Honecker, the head of the German Democratic Republic, when the leader was on state visits and no other interpreter would take up the challenge or endure the risk of helping such an unpopular statesman make himself understood. I questioned him about his allegiance, to which he replied: "I know, Honecker was a little – how should I say – *different*, but I figured a revolutionary who married his prison warden nine years his senior must have a rich inner life. Maybe he was just an acquired taste."

I was never a communist, but we intuitively took a dislike to the same people, without ever acknowledging or dwelling on it, there was no need: I could tell from the way his voice quickly morphed into a dull hiss before he coldly crucified them, often in public. I would quietly relish that deconstruction, enjoy it as some form of art, a minimalistic performance of the highest caliber. We were members of the same unspoken, unofficial, unrecognized *Internationale*, that went beyond political parties or personal beliefs and

DANIEL SOHA

connected a few dotty, fundamentally rebellious individuals in an almost occult manner.

He was strong and he was intelligent, so his demise was a long, painful process, from fight to fight, from one fallback line to the next.

His successor in Beirut, a notoriously incompetent fellow who kept being promoted because cutting him off from end constituents was the best way the system could find to prevent him from causing irreparable damage, eventually got into trouble: money missing, "creative" accounting and the like. Naturally, he put the blame on his predecessor. The Parisian office sent three goons in their darkest suits to investigate the matter, and they found copies of the personal cheques clumsily written out to Jacques – and not to his administration – by Mother Superior.

It was a no-no, even though Jacques proved quite unequivocally that he did not appropriate a single penny, and the funds would immediately be returned to the Treasury. It did not matter. They needed a culprit, so their job could be completed and they would perpetrate other miscarriages of justice.

Jacques' fate spiraled down – in stages, from defeats to counterattacks, never straight down but down all the same. He calmly and methodically prepared his defense: after all, he was in a very strong position, or so he thought. First and foremost, he did not do anything dishonest; besides, in times of war, extraordinary procedures can and have to be adopted to face seemingly impossible situations; also, the ultimate objective: to have the French government recover its funds in the middle of utter chaos, was met beyond expectations; and lastly, the French ambassador to Lebanon himself ordered him to proceed as he did.

His many letters and reports fell on deaf ears: too many powerful idiots he crucified, too many times in public. The ex-Ambassador corroborated his statement, but he had retired and his word no longer carried any weight.

Jacques was called to Paris, plane ticket and hotel paid. They ushered him into a little room with one table and one chair, and twelve large boxes of documents. When he asked them what they were, they answered: "This is your file, Sir. You can consult it at your leisure. Take your time." He was not allowed to use a photocopy machine or take.

Meanwhile, back in Singapore, his "allies" were becoming increasingly distant: even with the best intentions, nobody wants to be associated with trouble. When the French Ambassador to the Lion State decided that the balance of power has shifted and it was safer to keep his distance, he withdrew the "unwavering" support he had promised.

One day, Jacques got official notice that his appointment was over. When he indicated that his son was two months away from high school graduation and could not possibly be taken to another continent, Jacques was told that he could stay in Singapore, but without pay and forbidden to tread the grounds of the French embassy. Banned from his own country, since the embassy actually was French territory.

This is when I performed what I still think was the most selfless and probably only heroic act of my life: with open contempt for the ominous forces at work and the consequences on myself and the world, I gave Jacques an office, a telephone and a secretary – and we sipped a bottle of Burgundy. As I recall, he drew on his pipe at the offer, made a sound like a kind of long snort, and for the first time I noticed his eyes: pale blue and huge behind his steaming glasses.

I had encouraged him to hire a lawyer and keep fighting. He did. And he won, several years later. There was no provision in the law to reinstate a fallen angel, and in that court, damages were not admissible.

****

Jacques and I kept corresponding after that. He took an early retirement and his health deteriorated steadily: a knee operation first, then a freakish heart condition. One day, when we were walking along a dreary coastline in the suburbs of Montpellier and he had to sit down every few steps because his knee was bending backward, I became convinced that the horror the system had inflicted upon him drilled a gaping hole in his heart that nothing could ever fill.

A blood disease was the next calamity that befell him, with increasingly frequent transfusions and no clear diagnosis. The hole was getting larger.

When he lost consciousness at his home, his wife and son called an ambulance, and they all went to emergency. One of the paramedics, an Arab who had been a surgeon in his own country but could not get recognition for his medical credentials in the French system, whispered cautiously that Jacques' red blood cells were disappearing at a record rate: "I've never seen anything quite like it. I'll be surprised if he's still alive when we reach the hospital."

But he was. Unconscious but alive.

Three or four hours later, well after nightfall, he suddenly sat up in bed and asked to see his wife and his son separately – "let's do it fast, I'm in a rush", he said. He spent 45 minutes with each, calm and collected, giving them recommendations and advice, then called them in together.

"Has the dog been fed?"

"No, we just rushed to the hospital as fast as we could."

"But the dog does not know what is happening, he has done nothing wrong, he doesn't understand. And you left him alone, hungry and scared! Go home immediately and feed him."

They did.

Jacques died right after they left.

Such was my friend Jacques.

If I Killed John McIntyre

To my daughter Lexi,
on her eighteenth birthday

If I killed the infamous John McIntyre, your Honour, it is because of my daughter's teddy bear.

No, your Honour, I am not mad: it's Martin's fault… but I have to go back to the beginning, so you can really understand what happened, put into perspective a chain of events that took almost thirty years to unfold. Only then will you have some of the key elements that will clarify this act of violence which the District Attorney has deemed a deliberate, cold-blooded crime.

When I first got married, in a bout of collective drunkenness which was frequent in her native Newfoundland, my mother-in-law jokingly gave me a brown teddy bear with short, slightly curly hair and a particularly sweet expression, calling upon my immaturity and obvious craving for affection, evidenced in my abducting her daughter. This jocular, eccentric Christmas gift was greeted with the laughs it deserved for as long as it deserved them, which was a few minutes. It was then put back into its box and taken to New York where we lived, and spent a few years on the highest shelf of a closet, at a height we could not reach.

My wife and I waited twelve years before we had children and moved to Canada, then to France and eventually to Asia.

Forgotten in his box, the teddy bear followed us faithfully and routinely in the cartons of our successive moves, a slumbering traveler patiently waiting to awaken in a world where he would be well-received and celebrated.

On her first Christmas, my daughter Lexi was six months old. It was at the beginning of December that the red and gold box where the bear had been kept came tumbling on my head, as I was groping in the dark for a hammer, a screwdriver or some other tool. I introduced the teddy bear to my mother who was then visiting, and she authoritatively called him Martin, on the grounds that "a bear cannot possibly be called anything else." I was quite moved by this collusion between two different mothers twelve years and thousands of miles apart, and gratefully accepted this epithet.

When I went against everybody's advice ("newborns don't have a sense of gifts or celebrations and the like") and placed Martin in my daughter's cradle on the morning of December 25, she gratified him with a long, bright smile loaded with joy and tenderness, took him effusively in her arms and started sucking on his ear. It only took her a few minutes to fall asleep, filled with affection. The relationship had been sealed.

Lexi and Martin soon became inseparable. She would often hold him by one arm and drag him along, clutch him in times of stress, and he would cushion her falls when she stubbornly ran in babies' shoes that were too wide, too thick, too stiff. At night, to put her to sleep, he would tell her those stories that only children can soak up through sight or touch, and my daughter's big eyes would take on a glassy look and eventually close, overwhelmed by such cuddly comfort.

One day, Martin lost an eye, and we looked everywhere but could not find it. Horrified by this mutilation, Lexi shrieked uncontrollably. Faced with such an emergency, my wife promptly grabbed a button out of her sewing kit and decided to sew it on the empty space the lost eye had left. She could only find an overcoat button, which was far too big and far too round, but for a mysterious reason this seemed to satisfy Lexi. Martin's physical look and expression were forever altered, but for Lexi things were back to normal, and she soon started treating Martin with her usual mix of consideration and carelessness, like "before the tragedy."

It was on one of our trips to Paris, back at our hotel at the end of the day, that we noticed Martin was not there. We looked everywhere and came to the painful realization that Lexi had forgotten him at one of the places we had visited. Her face bathed in tears, she made a superhuman effort for a child her age to come to terms with the consequences of her mistake and told me in a broken voice: "I will be brave, daddy." Caught in the waves and heaves of her first big sorrow, she eventually fell asleep, sobbing well into the middle of her tormented dreams.

People say that I am a monster, that I have no conscience, that I am incapable of remorse or compassion, a murderer, nastiest among the nasty. Would such an evil man have done what I did on that day? With hazy eyes and a quivering chin, I left in a tizzy and, hopping from one cab to another in hellish traffic, I followed in reverse the itinerary of the whole day. Greengrocers and museum attendants were mercilessly interrogated while I gazed at them with a demented look on my face; a pimply choir boy, then a young priest and maybe even an archbishop had to submit to my questioning in Notre-Dame cathedral. In the midst of a stunned crowd, I heard myself describe the lost entity to an incredulous policeman: "Yes, a teddy bear, this big, with one eye bigger than the other."

It was in an art shop on the West Bank where I eventually ended up, helpless and in total exhaustion, that the clerk announced with a smile: "I'll bet you that a little girl you know has forgotten something", and triumphantly pulled Martin out from under the counter. The look of wonder and admiration that Lexi gave me the next day when she awoke next to Martin is forever etched in my memory, it will stay with me until I die. It is a look for which I would have killed, for which I would still kill. Come to think of it, it is a look for which I *did* kill.

The days and the nights then paraded along, too short and unstoppable, and Martin followed all the episodes of Lexi's childhood, then of her teen years, with his crazy half-wink, witnessing those evenings when she would collapse into her bed after four or five hours of dance classes or demoralized by some routine confrontation at school, and those crisp mornings when she would wake up with the certainty that everything was possible, that the world was her apple. Martin was the confidant of all her girlie secrets and all her innermost hopes that she would whisper in his ear when we no longer knew how to listen. She never parted from him; he would join her on her sleepovers, and nobody even thought of poking fun, as it was obvious that there was something there which went beyond the comprehension, the sensitivity or the conventions displayed by the bottom feeders of the human race. Lexi got rounder, shapelier, she filled in, and her first boyfriends, then her first lovers followed each other in quick succession in her room where the posters of the Back Street Boys or the Spice Girls had suddenly disappeared.

Unchanged and unfazed, Martin sometimes seemed to wink maliciously in the shadowy light where the musky fragrance of pleasure was still floating. The portraits of her gentlemen friends had changed a few times over on her night table when we put our meager resources behind her stellar future and sent her to study in the United States. Martin, who had always been around, followed her there. It was obvious, no discussion!

It was at that point that the horrid John McIntyre appeared on the scene.

John McIntyre III, that swine, was the third in his dynasty. The latest brat in a lineage of plutocrats who had made a fortune selling rubber hoses, he struck me as the personification of stupidity and arrogance in a relatively stately young man, tall, well-built and handsome – a turd with blond hair.

Of course, your Honour, you know perfectly well that a father feels rather personally affected when a hairy thing, a hypersexual entity, invades the privileged space that he believes he shares exclusively with his daughter, but it was much more than that: Lexi had had other boyfriends, and the transition had been smooth – I was even complacent at times! What was particularly shocking about this one? Probably the permanent feeling of crass stupidity, which is always irritating, but also, and most of all, the faint but pervasive feeling that in his case, intelligence in any form, albeit non-existent in this particular instance, was not even required for survival. And neither were manners, kindness, consideration, or even the conventions that placate on the social fabric a harmonious – or at least peaceful – front.

And then, of course, there was also this discomfort which all men feel in the presence of women they loved, whether they are spouses, daughters or mothers, when they have left them for someone else: how could she give herself to this chump? With this kind of outlook you can easily find yourself at the edge of cynicism and contempt, and you have to fend off those negative thoughts or you may sink into despair. And believe me, your Honour, I did fend them off, every inch of the way, I repressed them, I tried my very best to find a redeeming spark in this John McIntyre, this fiend, this rat!

I put myself through unspeakable humiliation, swallowed every ounce of pride I had. I caught myself grimacing a half a smile when this windbag boasted of feats of seduction or casually described the odd fluxes and impulses of that parallel world, so real and obvious to him, where money had no meaning. I said nothing when he treated all those who are dear to me as his personal servants, or when he publicly lost his temper, in a restaurant where I had invited him to get to know him better, because his champagne cocktail was too slow coming. For my daughter, for a glimmer in her big beautiful eyes, I would have lit his cigar with my last fifty-dollar bill.

But it is something completely different that sealed the fate of John McIntyre, that scum! I had noticed very early on that Lexi came back from the evenings she spent with him in an extreme state of fatigue and nervousness, at times with red marks on her wrists or on her arms. I eventually enquired about it, and after I strongly insisted, her only reply was stubborn, grievous silence, except for a few words referring to the anger-prone, authoritative, uncontrollable nature of "John" ... how dare she call him that, that sack of dung, that subspecies! For all my sadness, I then felt enormous relief: the circumstances of her seduction, her mistakes in judgment, her self-delusions had become irrelevant. She was unhappy and afraid of him. Again, she needed me.

If one day I stayed hidden in a nook of her small apartment waiting for them, I didn't mean to hurt anyone – no, your Honour, it was just to protect her! Originally, I wanted to witness what was going to happen, check whether he was beating her, and then I would burst on the scene, show my determination, chase away the intruder. I was expecting a grandiose, vibrant, melodramatic scene and I could see myself playing Zeus the Almighty with lightning bolts in my hands, I had a scenario for every possible situation, a reply to every outrageously stupid remark that John McIntyre, that jackass, would undoubtedly blurt out, and I imagined him retreating in shame, forever losing face.

Instead of all that, what I witnessed was a mediocre, pathetic, hopeless scene, on a pretense so ludicrous that it had better be left unspoken, and which John McIntyre, that putz, had blown out of proportion to cater to his domineering urges. He barked and barked again, all the more noisily as he felt increasingly powerless, stamped the floor with his foot; it was childish, harmless, as though he thought money had bought him the right never to be contradicted: sooner or later she would dump him, she would make him bite the dust, I was sure of it, and this whole episode would be forgotten. From my hiding place, I only saw Lexi in three-quarter profile, crying softly and holding Martin against her.

I was wondering whether I should even come out to put an end to this pitiful scene, when suddenly I saw John McIntyre, that abomination, stretch out his arm angrily and grab Martin; I saw my daughter desperately try and hold on to a handful of fluff; I saw Martin torn apart. Maybe all the straw and cotton that flew around made me lose my mind for a brief moment, but I thought I suddenly saw, in the midst of all the debris, the look of grief and despair that had devastated me many years before, in a Paris hotel room: the look that made me do the impossible in a moment of love so beautiful that, whatever your verdict is, it will bring me Heaven's best consideration. I also saw in my mind, as clearly as I am seeing you now, that *other* look which, early the next morning, had sealed my new status as *Le Magnifique*, a knight in shining armour, a prince forever charming in the eyes of a little girl. So I stepped out of the dark with the paperweight in my hand.

If I killed John McIntyre, that crud, it is not because of what he was or what he stood for, however much I hated it;

neither is it out of love for my daughter, or not entirely; it was not even to prove to the world, in a twisted, over-inflated way, this trivial truth: there are times when a teddy bear from the dollar store is worth more than all the gold in the world.

If I killed John McIntyre, third and last of his dynasty, your Honour, it is with a motive that I fear will not add much favour for me in your judicial system.

It is because Martin did not deserve to die.

Family Matters

J ani left Hungary after the war, hidden in the tender of a steam locomotive, too young to be politicized but young enough to run, away from the starvation communism was imposing on its children. He settled in France, and now, twenty years later, he goes back with a wife and a son in tow, driving a little Simca. He was invited by his brother, a member of the Communist Party who visited him a year before in France. Although Jani left his country illegally, his brother made sure that he would not be arrested or prosecuted, or so he said. Still, Jani shakes a little. His nervousness shows at the border. They ask him to get out of the car, they interrogate him. They interrogate Etel too. And little David. David is thirteen, he no longer speaks Hungarian very well, he started to forget the language deliberately at the age of six, when he started school, to prove to all those French bullies that he could be more French than them if he wanted to. They interrogate the whole family first, then each member separately, to see if they will contradict each other. The process lasts two, three hours. Every fifteen minutes or so, they disappear behind an opaque glass door, pick up a big black polymer phone, report back to Budapest. Jani tries to eavesdrop, overhear, interpret their expression if he can, read their lips when they go to the end of the hallway and start whispering to each other. Etel has put on her dogged, mildly indignant look and David fancies himself in a Humphrey Bogart movie: "A tough cookie, that kid!" "Yeah, but he'll spill the beans, they all do…" So he smiles. He can't take those torturer's apprentices seriously: two young men who do not look like they find much pleasure in what they do, who are visibly sick of the cult of secrecy, dressed in grey uniforms in a grey building when a few feet away is Austria and the merry yodelling of big-breasted walküries in the haystacks. It is with an uncomfortable smile that the two young men finally release Jani and his family, apologetically stammering some excuse just in case Jani would complain to his brother or to some other person of influence. "You understand, we had to check!…" It's already night-time and Jani starts speeding up on a concrete highway that must have been built for tanks and armoured vehicles. He is reluctant to speak, maybe they put listening devices in the car. There are no lights and no other vehicles on the road, only occasionally the reflector of a bicycle that dances like a red firefly before disappearing on a roadside trail. Between each concrete slab the car jolts a little. Dudum. Dudum. For the next 200 kilometers.

Jani's brother Zoltán is jovial and chubby, each time he laughs his belly shakes like a bowl of jelly. It is a sign of prosperity in this country, it means that the regime feeds you well and you have been groomed for success. When he visited France a year ago he asked Jani: "Where are the fat people? Are you hiding them?" But he is charming, intelligent, a free thinker in his own way – and of course, within reason. Nothing you might expect from an apparatchik. At the end of the war, when opportunism reigned supreme and all Western powers were welcoming the brain drain from eastern Europe because it proved their ideological superiority, he chose to stay, he had that courage. Or that carelessness.

The Party spotted him very early. He was a coal miner's son born into a large family, intelligent, honest and loyal, so he ticked all the right boxes. The Party took him under its wings, sponsored him, funded him, helped him and propelled him to the highest honours, and even forgave him for his sense of humour. All he had to do was become a member. Zoltán owes the Party his life, and the Party owes him an image of benevolence and kindness, and real competence in economic matters, which is good for the nation.

Discussions between Jani and Zoltán are animated but devoid of animosity, they each see the other's point of view. France welcomed the fugitive and let him alight smoothly in a land of plenty, the regime's pet was rewarded for his courage and his loyalty, and all the rhetoric ends up dissolving in large swigs of *pálinka*. They both meet the morning after in the kitchen trying to massage their scalps and mumbling: "*jaj! Olyan fáj a fejem!*" (Ouch! I have such a headache!), and the conversation starts again. The women try to give their two cents' worth, but they are being stared at with total incomprehension, even compassion. Don't they understand that those matters only men, and only brothers, can discuss?

Zoltán is the CEO of an entire coal mining basin, he's a very big wig. He visits his empire every day, goes from one mine to the other, listens to everybody, seems to know them all by name, thousands of them. He pinches cheeks, pulls earlobes, kisses babies, follows up on families, careers, births, weddings and funerals. The people like him. They trust him. He's a local boy, they feel the closeness, and even though he is a Party dignitary, he does not ramble in Newspeak too much or clap his hands too long at other people's ramblings.

But family life is another story. Inexplicably at first, the air is heavy, the meals are strangely quiet, the weight of the untold is paralyzing. Then, little by little, through discreet hints and indirect references to the past at first, some light is shed on the situation. As days go by, the pálinka is lifting the fog, or rather clearing it to replace it with its own haze, and confidential stuff comes out all the more readily because everybody has forgotten it the next day – or almost.

Ten years earlier, deceived by Khrushchev's liberal rhetoric, Hungary rebelled against its Stalinist regime. At first, the five Soviet divisions stationed in the country tried to repress the rebellion, but they ended up befriending the insurgents and withdrawing. A few days later, claiming that they were fighting a neo-nazi insurrection, the Russians sent 200 000 Tatars, Turkmen, Buryats or Chechens from their most remote steppes – an ethnic choice imposed by the fear that an excessive cultural closeness might prompt that second repressive wave to fraternize once more with the enemy.

But even before the first wave withdrew, Zoltán's wife Ilona had fled and reached the Austrian border, with two children in her arms and one in her belly. Zoltán refused to leave and stayed in his big house all by himself, ready to confront whomever wanted to ask him about his deeds and renege on his allegiance to the Communist Party. A coal miner's son, he was nothing and owed the Party everything: his studies, his profession, his perks, his beautiful house and his chauffeur, even if the latter had mysteriously disappeared. His loyalty was not negotiable, especially since he had always tried to do the right thing, in the name of socialism and of its ideal of justice and humanity, of which he was one of the first beneficiaries. Zoltán was an honest man. He had never made compromises or jeopardized his principles, never demeaned himself in front his superiors or been contemptuous or condescending to his subordinates.

At the news that the second wave of Soviet invaders had crossed the border, Hungarians released their wrath against the members and the supporters of the Communist Party, who were considered as collaborationists and accused, by a twist of fate, of being lackeys and enforcers of Russian imperialism. In the plush residential neighbourhood where Zoltán lived, he sometimes heard screaming, clamours, then deathly silence. And he kept on waiting, ready to explain, not knowing or refusing to believe that if someone knocked at his door, it would not be to ask for explanations, that the time for explanations was all but gone.

Nobody came.

Had he been forgotten? Did everybody presume that he had left with his family or that he wouldn't dare to stay, show that arrogance, be that insane? Or was he simply respected by the workers – a social class from which he came and which he never abandoned or mistreated? He never found out.

Jani asks to see his other brothers and sisters and his childhood friends. No problem to see family or relatives, although nobody else seems to have joined the Communist Party, so in Zoltán's presence they are rather cold and distant. But about former friends, Zoltán seems to be more reticent, he always finds a pretense or an excuse, usually that he didn't know what happened to them or that they went to the West in 1956. But he's lying, that's obvious. So Jani comes up with a plan.

At lunch time, Zoltán makes it a point to prove to his brother that there are no shortages in the country, so he treats him with wholesome foods, like a *bableves*, a bean soup with a roux and hot peppers fried in goose fat, or *fasírozott*, which are fried meat balls, and for dessert Ilona often prepares *palacsinta* crêpes or *csöröge*, those donuts twisted into bow-like shapes, and all those dishes are quite heavy, so they need two or three glasses of red wine to wash them down, and then at least a couple of slugs of apricot brandy. Before the end of the meal, Zoltán is already incoherent, he starts singing pre-war dirty songs and old Gypsy chants, while Jani has only pretended to drink but hardly touched the stuff. As soon as Zoltán staggers away to have his afternoon nap, Jani takes his car and goes to visit his friends. No comment when he comes back: he simply went "on a drive", and socialism would be hard-pressed to begrudge him for this liberty, which routinely accompanies equality and fraternity in the official motto of the French republic.

One day, very early in the morning, Jani, Etel and David sneak out, just leaving a note on the kitchen counter. *"Don't worry. We'll be back. We are just sightseeing."* They are off to see Etel's aunt, her father's sister. József lived in Canada and the United States, but has spent the last forty years in France and has not seen or heard from Katalin in a half a century. Jani has promised him that he would try and find her to give her a letter that József has spent the last year to write – ever since he found out that Jani was planning a trip to Hungary.

She lives in a small village by the Ukrainian border – a place she has never left, from the time she was hired as a farmer's servant seven miles away from where her parents, relatives and friends lived. After the Great War, her village of birth got partitioned off to Ukraine and she was the only family member who remained on the "right" side of the border: in Hungary, but stranded and alone.

David will always remember her extreme poverty, her indigence, almost nun-like. Katalin lives in a small room with curved walls and twisted angles, almost a Gypsy's caravan, with no ornaments, no trinkets, no embellishments, just a wooden crucifix on the wall, a wood stove in a corner, a straw mattress in another, a few blackened aluminum pots, and somewhere else in the room one wobbly chair and a little table. She greets her visitors with embarrassment, almost annoyance. Why on earth have they come to track her down? How dare they? How could she possibly be of any interest to anyone, to the point of even taking a few minutes of their time? She is a dignified old lady dressed in black, with her heard carried oddly high while reflecting the despondency of an unnecessary life spent in lonely hardships. Still, she looks proud and single-minded, it is obvious that she makes it a point to keep her environment immaculately clean, maybe because cleanliness is what's the closest to godliness.

And she is not a Gypsy: she has never stolen anything, not even food. David is only thirteen years old but he finds her almost beautiful in her useless dignity, he tries to read in her faded eyes the unspeakable sadness she must have endured, to imagine her solitude, with no family and no husband. She has not seen her brother in fifty years, she was a servant until she was forced into retirement by the government. What does she live on? Nobody knows, not even József, and Jani does not dare to ask.

When she hears that these foreigners have come a thousand miles just to convey the affection of her brother and give her a letter, she does not move, just holds the sealed envelope in her hand and starts crying silently. She does not ask any questions, wants no news, no feedback, the emotion is enough, she barely listens to the stories Jani is telling her to avoid the oppression of silence. Through her tiny window, she looks at the Simca on the trail by the forest and shows no expression, no comprehension: that machine is so far from what she knows, from what she's ever known! She asks them to sit on the straw mattress, looks at David. So he's her grand-nephew? A new misty wave clouds her eyes.

She does not have anything to offer, not even a slice of *beigli* or a piece of that infamous Polish chocolate that socialist Europe has learned to enjoy. In her closet, she finds a little box of tea with some dusty Russian Akbar and a few cups with finely chiselled handles, of surprising elegance in that environment.

She does not have a tray, so she serves tea on an old hardboard panel with flaky corners. From where he is sitting on the straw mattress, Jani vaguely sees a shape, like some illustration painted on the back of the panel. He leans further down, tries to have a better view. She notices. He asks her what it is, and if she could show it. She is a little reticent a first, then with a coy "oh, it's nothing", she puts the cups on the little table, turns the panel over and clumsily holds the picture up, a little askew.

— It's a Rembrandt!

Of course, it is not. It is the portrait of a lovely young girl whose luminous face pierces the darkness created by six decades spent macerating in the soot and the fat of a crude makeshift kitchen, blackened like the backs of its pots and pans. The young girl exhibits a little pout, quite enigmatic, but not like Mona Lisa's blissfully calm half-smile, just a vague look of discontent, like she had been forced to pose and did not want to. Stubborn but infinitely graceful, with a beauty that's all the more poignant that she is extraordinarily unaware of it, and certainly ignorant of the effect it would still produce in another world aeons later.

What's this? Who's that girl? Jani is flabbergasted.

It is a portrait of Katalin that was painted when she was fifteen years old by one of those wandering artists that roamed the Austro-Hungarian empire, sleeping in barns and eating whatever locals gave them for a drawing or a painting of their favourite landscapes or their loved ones. As years went by, with that total lack of sentimentality that characterizes many poor people, Katalin had lost any attachment to what she considered like a worthless smudge, but for some reason she had never thrown it out, using it instead for the virtues of the hardboard itself, either as a wedge to keep her door open or as a flat surface to write some mail on. Today, it serves as a tray.

Jani asks her why she does not seem attached to it. She gives him a blank look, obviously does not understand the question. He says that he would like to take it off her hands if she will let him. For a price, of course. For the first time, she laughs a little. It is bad manners to rip off relatives by selling them worthless items, no, she will give it to him since he wants it, she insists, puts it in his hands.

He refuses. He takes a handful of banknotes and coins out of his pocket, French and Hungarian all mixed up, he does not want to count, he does not care about the value – a paltry sum for a Rembrandt, puts the money on the table. She does not budge. She does not understand. He slowly makes his way to the door with Etel and David, wishes her all the blessing of Heaven, Hungarian-style, respectfully kisses her hand before he leaves, tries to say a few affectionate words. *Csókolom. IstenÁgyom meg.*

How long will those few bucks make her live a better life? Maybe she will get herself some nice food on the black market, maybe she will buy a coat or two for the winter, a bottle of wine from time to time? It will last her for months, for sure, it is an exorbitant sum for her, he sees it on her face, she looks aghast and deeply moved at the same time, she's never seen so much money, especially banknotes, since the last time her brother József came to see her on his way back from the Americas.

When the Simca pulls out, Katalin makes a little gesture with her hand. She is crying. Jani too.

Cousin Ashlyn

Forty years have passed since my marvelous, tragic encounter with the world of the Sidh. And in those forty years, you have believed nothing but the mediocre, pathetic illusion of your senses, able to see only as far as the tip of your science. And still, you persistently claim that my tortured psyche had been overcome by a brain fever all those years ago, somewhere between Black Head and Moher, in Clare County, and that it created cousin Ashlyn out of nothing. How can you then explain that I can still see her, hear her, feel her so vividly? Why should her features have remained so deeply etched in my memory, with all their endless subtleties and the fleeting, unfathomable depth of their expression? How dare you suggest that there might be no reason at all for my addiction to the substances that I ingest, while they are specifically intended to keep me in a state of grace, ready to blend in with the People of the Night? Have you not understood yet? Must I explain again?

Why I decided one day to pay a visit to old Meaghan remains a mystery lost in the twists and turns of my own early life. I was twenty years old, the college year was coming to an end and, as many young men living in the British Isles, I was stifled by insularity and dreaming of faraway travels, of losing myself in exotic places. The person we called "Aunt Meaghan", although she was but a distant relative, was the only member of our family who did not leave Ireland before the Great War. I had never seen her, but my mother, who was a good ten to twelve years younger, still remembered her radiant beauty and proud demeanour, fit for a poet's heart and dreams. Every four or five years, we would get from her a few tightly, elegantly handwritten pages in the old language, mindless trifles expressed in obsolete, touching words. A lone orphan, she obstinately clung to the Burren in a little thatch-roofed stone house facing the ocean and proclaimed with feverish eyes to whomever would listen that she would never leave because she was going to "uncover the secret". There were no questions asked: that world was aloof and famished and did not talk much; and besides, mystery, strangeness, magic would nestle in each of its stony nooks and routinely paint themselves in the gigantic whirls of its waters and of its skies, which displayed at times Nature's most exquisite flamboyance, and at times its darkest moods.

I had always been attracted to the unusual and fascinated by our family legend which people kept recounting in instinctively hushed tones; I was further obsessed with the obscure urge to reconnect with roots that I felt were getting more distant in my perception and my memory. After I had sent several unanswered letters to Meaghan, I decided one day to leave industrial Lancashire where I had been residing and headed for Ireland. It was in mid-April and the weather had become more pleasant. My constitution, already rather frail, must have started its long decline, as I recall being afflicted by frequent dizzy spells that would split my field of vision and leave me with horrendous migraines. But to be entirely truthful, as many people of Irish descent, I was consuming whiskey with quasi religious fervor, for I also believed that I was a great poet and was therefore convinced that I would not live to be thirty.

Of the journey I have kept no memory. My mind has now become totally uncompromising and self-absorbed, but even then, I had a tendency to by-pass all the petty details that were not immediately feeding my deepest obsessions. It is only much later, in the course of my long illness, that people found in my pockets the ticket stubs that enabled them to reconstruct the itinerary which had taken me by bus and ferry from Bolton to Liverpool, then to Dublin and Galway. However, I do recall walking through the mountains and along the lakes of the Connemara region, then following the coast of Black Head, where a meager, yellowish moor flanks a ragged rocky coastline in which umpteen rainfalls have created deep furrows and odd patterns. South of Black Head, the coast progressively rises and turns into a cliff, and one suddenly gets the feeling that the rocks are standing straight, that the world has flipped to conform to esoteric laws, just like a Moebius strip with no inside or out. There, the winds are so strong that the rain falls upward, the sky is green and the grass is blue. This was where aunt Meaghan lived.

I arrived there at nightfall, drenched and chilled by the mist that had soaked me through the whole day. I feared and maybe hoped for the worst, but it was a handsome old lady with an air of great intelligence that opened the door. I introduced myself and she invited me with an engaging smile to come by the fireplace and warm up. The ensuing conversation was routinely courteous, but slow and hesitant, not only because she was reluctant to speak English and my Gaelic was not too fluent, but mostly because, as I felt, she was not too used to talking, and neither did she have a taste for it. She heated up a pot on the cast iron stove and handed me a huge plate steaming with potato stew; reading my thoughts, she then casually remarked with her back turned: "There was a day when potatoes were a luxury in these parts", and with no apparent reason, she went on: "Your cousin Ashlyn will be back later." She did not react to the look of surprise that I must have cast and gave me an opaline cup: "Here, drink!" The extreme bitterness of the herbal tea almost made me nauseous, but I attempted not to show it and thanked her profusely. At ten, I suddenly felt a wave of exhaustion come over me. Silently, Meaghan took me to a little whitewashed attic room.

I have no recollection about falling asleep: it seems to me that I just crashed into a marvelous dream which I felt had begun well before, like a motion picture that one joins after it has started. A lost traveler in a flat, monotonous moor, I was attracted to the chants of a remote chorus with strange accents which could be heard in the distance, and found myself in front of a cliff, the marble of which was also the walls of a monumental place of worship, its huge spire lost in the clouds. Entering this fabulous cathedral, I walked through a pagan crowd chanting a word I could not make out. Little by little, the singing grew louder, the chorus turned into a saraband, and I discovered with unspeakable joy that I was chanting in unison the name of...

"... Ashlyn. I am Ashlyn."

I rubbed my eyes, still permeated by the magic of my dream. The girl who was looking at me from the threshold of my bedroom, bare-footed in a white nightgown, was of luminous beauty, the like of which I had never seen before and would never see again. Her long black hair circled the perfect oval of her face with exquisite harmony; and yes, her huge, bluish-green eyes gave her a look of sublime unreality; and indeed, the freshness of her complexion, the grace of her gait, the charm of her smile were moving me to distraction, yet there was more to it: each new expression as she spoke, each new configuration of her body as it slowly moved towards me, each glimmer that my flickering oil lamp projected on her revealed new aesthetic depths and triggered rapture a thousand fold, like those seafaring sunrises which are different every day, yet always magnificent. Flabbergasted, my heart bare, I then knew that I was hopelessly in love, that I had always loved her, even before I met her, even before I wiggled myself free, all bloody and wailing, out of my mother's flesh.

She sat at the bottom of my bed, talked to me for hours in her cool, melodious voice, at times in the old tongue whose rough tones she handled with infinite grace and poetry, and at times in a softly hissing form of English, the consonants of which she caressed with the tip of her tongue. She told me the story of the seafaring Fomoires, those horrendous, demonic giants who had landed in Ireland right after the Flood, she told me about the Partholonians who, before the priests, before even the druids, had populated the known world in its entirety and whose descendants had founded the cities of Tyre, Carthage and Uxmal, about that nation of demigods that erected at the dawn of humanity thousands of colossal megaliths as a tribute to the third son of Noah who had initiated it; she told me about the war with the Fomoires, about Nemed, Senlon and Beothach. She told me with passion, pointing at her magnificent face, that she originated from this people, these divine alchemists and brewers. She claimed that she was the descendant of Tuan MacCairill the mutant, only survivor of the disaster that buried his race, and who then impregnated the Spanish-born women of the Milesians, who were human themselves but had defeated the Tuatha, last gods of Ireland. She told me about the defeat of those gods, forbidden to die and who therefore took refuge in the parallel universe of the Sidh, beyond the horizon of the sea. She told me she would take me there, she told me she knew the secret. And I was lulled by her mermaid voice, captivated by her sorcery. I adored her instantly. At the break of dawn, she left without a sound, and a discreet aroma of lilacs and almonds lingered in the room.

The next few days followed the same routine: I would sleep most of the day away, then exchange a few words with old Meaghan who would feed me one of her brews and make me drink her revolting herb tea. I would then sleep for a few minutes and have superb dreams, and Ashlyn would wake me up and talk to me until daybreak, then disappear. She told me one night that May 1 was the day of Beltrane, when the Sidh came in contact with the real world and the People of the Night – fairies, elves and gods that humanity had repelled out of fear and ignorance-showed itself to a chosen few in celebration of the Spring, carrying them into their swirling dance. And I did not know what to think, I wondered whether Ashlyn was mad or officiating as a poet or a witch, but I nevertheless let myself carried away by the wonder of her tales, I would wholeheartedly adhere to her fantasies, I was surrendering without even resisting. Indeed, I must have been ill already, because my brain did not react to all of this strangeness, it was content feeding off her, the living source of desire and beauty, and getting inebriated. I had become dependent on the form and increasingly avid for the substance.

I do not recall when I told her I loved her. I remember that she smiled and this smile made my heart jump, and one night her linen dress fell on the floor, heavy as silk. I will always remember the embrace, the plunge into many layers of unspeakable bliss, an ecstatic, endless spiral where the universe had miraculously reorganized itself around us, the absorption of my whole being into hers. What I remember is that I possessed beauty itself and united with it for a brief eternity, I remember growling, crying, burning myself deliciously in its heat. I remember her husky, barbaric pleasure, her gleaming, wild delight, at once tender and violent, her glance that was both aloof and penetrating, her half-closed eyes and the abandonment I was seeing in them. I remember that everything was clean and beautiful, that our gestures were delicate and considerate, that our senses had swollen with fulfillment and our hearts were overflowing with unspeakable intensity. I remember thinking that there could not possibly be a tomorrow and I would probably have to die, and I was ready for it.

It is a little while thereafter that my dreams began eluding my control, that I no longer had the strength to contain them, that they started oozing, then pouring into the real world. Imperceptibly, the crowd in my marble basilica had become silent, then hostile, and one night I thought I saw goats' feet, rams' horns, grimacing midgets, then the large white walls began to crack, hideous dragons appeared and cursed me in a cavernous voice, their mouths filled with black smoke. My sleep became increasingly agitated and feverish, I ended up living in a state of perpetual exhaustion, of prostrated semi-slumber, and I would no longer leave my bed very much, and aunt Meaghan would silently bring me her beverages to make me stronger. On the eve of Beltrane, Ashlyn slipped into my bed and I greeted her in tears, embraced her with all the fervour I could summon in my state of despair. I shrieked in horror when suddenly, before my eyes, her body turned into something primeval and unmentionable, and I heard her spew the worst imprecations, the most vulgar, most obscene words, laughing in a way that turned my blood to ice. I caught my head in my hands, and when I dared look again in her direction there was nothing but beautiful, sweet Ashlyn, and her bluish-green eyes were looking at me with puzzlement and tenderness. I told her what I had seen. She said nothing, looked at me sadly, touched my cheek with her hand, kissed me tenderly.

Beltrane came, and that night I did not sleep. I looked all over for old Meaghan, but she had seemingly vanished. Around midnight, I heard muffled voices, chuckles, and Ashlyn's voice calling me. When I looked out the window, I staggered and had to lean against the wall not to faint in terror and helplessness. Oh indeed Ashlyn was there, swanlike, magnificent, in all her divine splendour, but she was surrounded by those demons which my dreams had forged and which had slipped into this world though the fractures of my weakened mind: sniggering devils, deformed dwarves, speaking animals, hybrid, repulsive creatures that the devil himself had conceived, the most hideous, terrifying, spectacle the world had even seen.

Ashlyn was calling me, desperately, holding her hand out: "Come, come forever with me to the world of the Sidh, do not believe just what you see, follow me, love me." I summoned all my courage, all my strength, screamed out my rejection, on the edge of consciousness. Ashlyn looked at me one last time, I saw in her expression an unusual harshness, and at that very moment it seemed to me for a split second that she was crying, before she disappeared, forever whisked away in a mad saraband, carried off by those monsters to which she had surrendered.

So you see, you wise academics, scholars of the world of medicine and psychiatry who have been studying my case diligently for decades, you are telling me that Ashlyn never existed, and that old Meaghan was found dead on the moor, in a white druid's robe, with an opaline cup in her hand. You are telling me that my monumental dreams and their nightmarish decay are typical of opium visions, you are telling me that the bitterness of the beverages I was administered was reminiscent of such hallucinogenic drugs as absinth and deadly night shade, that this bitterness and this bitter almond smell could even be akin to the murderous arsenic of the alchemists. Lastly, you have pointed out that Ashlyn is a deformation of the Irish word for *dream*, and told me about that legend from the Burren plateau, of young men dying every year in the Spring, dwelling in their delirious agony on a mysterious beauty of the moor. I understand all that and I respect your clumsy yearning for the truth. But please understand my certainty, for you know that if I had to resign myself to your interpretation, I would have no other recourse than suicide.

What I know is that Ashlyn lived with me, *inside* me for a few days, that she opened just for me a forbidden door and showed me ineffable treasures that only a few beings endowed with the highest form of sensitivity could behold, and that I betrayed her out of cowardice – that I refused, in fear of the monsters I had created in my own imagination, to follow her into that divine dimension where we would live an eternal love. But I know one day she will come back to me, even if, as she told me, a single day in the universe of the gods is like a whole year of life in the human world. I only hope that she will not be too long, that she misses me as much as I miss her. For you see, you wise scholars, despite my age, my frailty, my receding hairline and my wobbly teeth, despite all the ravages I imposed on my body, despite the drugs and the alcohol, I am still waiting for her and I will wait for her forever, I am waiting for her to come back sacrilegiously and unveil for me the secrets of the gods, erase all those years of hell that I endured for a second of weakness…

For with all my agonizing mind, I love her.

For better or for worse,
Whether angel or succubus,
Enlightened or insane,
An enchantress
or a witch,

I love her.

Maid in the USA

I will always remember the first time I saw Everett coming out of the fitness center of the American Club in Singapore: sweaty and jovial, covered front and back with a coarse reddish fuzz that a tank top too short to cover his solid belly was powerless to contain. He greeted me the American way, with a beaming, congenial smile, perfectly innocent and genuinely radiant. His head was like a massive latex mask of the Laughing Cow, never down, always upbeat. Our wives had become friends at my Juli's initiative, as she found the company of North Americans refreshing after several inbred years of French expat life among three million stolid Asians whose thoughts were impenetrable and actions incomprehensible.

At the age of 39, Everett Hodson III was the last offspring in a dynasty of Pittsburgh industrialists who had made a fortune selling construction nails at a cheaper price than anyone else. Everett had been sent to Singapore by his father to run the Asian subsidiary of Hodson Nails, got fired for unknown reasons, sued his "employer" for unlawful dismissal and brilliantly won a juicy settlement. But that was business, and it never prevented the family from getting together and saying grace at Thanksgiving. When I knew him, Everett was "in between jobs", pretending to live dangerously and regularly giving his virility a vigorous handshake for overcoming again and again the hardships that life had put in his way.

He met 45-year-old Sheila Hodson, *née* Doyle, in San Francisco where she ran a health food store. They sank into an unbridled vegetarian debauchery from which they only emerged to get married. They then settled down somewhat and widened their culinary horizons to include poultry, fish and seafood but no further, on the grounds that they could not eat an entity that had a face and four legs. I tried to serve them barbecued sausages for dinner one day, forcefully claiming that I had never seen a sausage with a face and four legs, but they would not have it. Speaking of food, it was Sheila who told us that one of the reasons why she was a Republican was that the United States was the only country in the world where the poor were fat. Cavalier, to say the least. They had a fertility issue, and after many attempts which included assisted reproductive technology, that misaligned, brazen American couple eventually farrowed a cross-eyed, cantankerous little turd I spontaneously nicknamed Sam-I-Am on account of his ragingly egotistical disposition. As was to be expected, he would shriek, stamp his feet and indiscriminately kick and punch everyone around him at the slightest annoyance, so our two little daughters and I never missed an opportunity to annoy him.

Like so many people for whom money is immaterial, Everett and Sheila had developed an immoderate taste for alcohol: fine wines for Everett and Champagne for Sheila. And as we had no pride at all, we shamelessly but thoroughly enjoyed the crumbs – or in this case the droplets – that fell from the table of their daily feasts, which to us was a horn of plenty. Sheila started guzzling after her afternoon shopping at 4 PM, and for her, two bottles of Roederer a day were not unusual. Thanks to Juli's emotional support and spirit of cooperation, at least an extra bottle was downed, while the men were savouring Château Margaux with flared nostrils and a pursed mouth. We would open our pieholes all the more willingly under their firkins because the Hodsons, who were already remarkably generous by nature, took it to heart to seal our newly found friendship by an unfailing and seemingly inexhaustible welcome. My only contribution to their lifestyle was to make them discover duck breasts: poultry that tastes like rare steak – a perfect sham to circumvent their taboos, like pastrami is beef that tastes like pork. Americans specialize in such make-believes and their hearts overflow with gratitude when you show them another forgery, another special effect.

Our honeymoon lasted over a year. Each day, we would go to bed light-hearted and slurring our goodnights, whenever we managed to stem the flow of spontaneous hatred our respective children were mutually displaying with charming sincerity. To reach that peace of mind, we had delegated the gruelling job of watching over the kids and keeping them under control to a discreet but ubiquitous feature of Singaporean life: the maid. The Filipina maid, a seamless institution in that regimented country, was unavoidable in the expat community, and for good reason: she cost one tenth the price of an apartment rental. There is a two-pronged diaspora from the Philippines: their glitzy singers supply reliable entertainment to all luxury hotels and leisure facilities from Japan to the Middle East, and their live-in housemaids, although somewhat less fortunate, still bring an important contribution to the revenue of the country. Indeed, even though the rental of an apartment in Singapore is ten times the compensation of a maid and even if in Hong Kong, space being at a premium, she sometimes has to sleep under the dining room table, the pittance she gets is still two or three times what she would make as a high school teacher in her own country. Are we good or evil when we take advantage of the system to exploit and oppress a human being while getting boundless gratitude in return? Better not ask.

To top it all, since we did not know where to start, we disgracefully hired our Diditt on physical criteria, talking ourselves into believing that our social status in the Lion State demanded we present the best possible image, in the interest of our beloved motherland which we absolutely had to represent in a dignified way.

In her community, Diditt was a superstar. Her head carried high and proud, her hair was flowing and heavy, her teeth were shiny and impeccably aligned, and everybody knew that she was a plantation owner's daughter who only had to seek additional income because of a sudden crash of the banana market. She was particularly admired by Lita, the Hodsons' maid: a skinny, concave creature with a yellowish complexion who dragged her feet from room to room in slow motion all day. Even more than ugliness, of which she had plenty, what emanated from her whole being was a kind of crushing sadness, and she would only liven up in the presence of Diditt, to whom she told mysterious stories in a hushed voice, using a rhythmic lingo punctuated by animated gesticulations. Everett was in awe ofDiditt's regal poise and asked me every day how I managed to find such a jewel, and I intimated that if money was within his purview, beauty was within mine.

We would become a little too cheerful right before dinner, and that was when Diditt and Lita would take care of the children, feed them and prevent them from exterminating each other, while the masters' banquet reached a humorous, convivial peak. Around eleven, the kids would fade, consumed by the intensity of their own resentment, and we would split into three groups, western women talking about western women's stuff, men drunkenly disclosing intimate secrets they would forget the next day, and maids probably pondering how ridiculous we all were.

From time to time, Everett let a bloodshot glance glide along Diditt's rump, then up and down her strong, suntanned legs, and he would just nod pensively, obviously reminiscing his deep discontent at the answer I gave him when he asked me, quite abruptly and unceremoniously, if I had humped her. "You mean she turns you on? You should be ashamed even to entertain such an idea", I replied, "and honestly, with your degree of affluence, you could be humping the most beautiful sarong girls in Singapore, chewing them up and spitting them out in style. Why would you want to add to the despondency and exploitation of a poor, penniless girl who's away from home and must feel miserable just being here?" He seemed to agree, but kept nodding dubitatively. Once, I heard him mutter: "This is crazy."

****

Our relationship reached a peak in alcoholic fantasy, consumerism and inconsequential partying, then slowly declined in successive stages. Maybe we were getting tired of a formula that had become a little stale and unimaginative, maybe we got sick of duck breasts, or maybe the intensity of a friendship whose exuberance was artificially amplified and maintained by the consumption of mentally corrosive substances was doomed to self-destruct. Or maybe, quite simply, Juli and I were beginning to feel uncomfortable at our inability to produce tokens of friendship that could match the Hodsons'. We were going to leave Singapore very soon, and the sorrow of our imminent departure barely obscured the fact that it was high time. We parted ways with a heavy heart and made the solemn promise that we would see each other again, no matter what, in Europe, North America or elsewhere, and left with tender, joyous memories of wild libations, lavish food and outright fun.

****

Over the next few months, our relationship became more distant but we kept the channels of communication open and would regularly call or write.

Inevitably, life just happened and we each went on to other pursuits: Diditt stayed with us a while, then moved back to Luzon, I got another job I didn't like in Toronto, Everett got deeply involved in nebulous business ventures, becoming first the CEO of an emerging welding company, then an internet wine merchant. Sheila fired poor Lita and sent her back to the Philippines after a mysterious altercation, then took her back apologetically a few weeks later. When asked about the circumstances of such a drastic episode, Sheila remained evasive, ultimately putting an abrupt end to the conversation with a categorical "I don't want to talk about it". Sam-I-Am the dunce flunked his last year of kindergarten and was kicked out of his luxurious private school for punching a little girl in her baby teeth, and rewarded by his parents with a one-million-dollar trust fund. Everything was hunky-dory.

A couple of years later, we got an invitation from the Hodsons. Would we like to spend our Christmas vacation with them in their spacious condo in Florida?

Would we indeed?

Wonderful, it would be like good old times again: mirth, seafood and alcohol abuse!

Well, think again.

Never try to recreate the past. I keep doing it and I am more disappointed every time. As soon as we arrived, we felt something was wrong, the air itself was sticky and thick, and had obviously been so for a while. The Hodsons were constantly on edge, overreacting for nothing, had all-round outbursts, but in a sneaky, civilized American way, without raising their voices too much, the nastiest insults being packaged in icy courtesy between long periods of caustic silence. "Something must have happened between them", whispers Juli. We try drinking, but this time it is dragging us even further down. Sam-I-Am is getting on my nerves more and more because he clearly has decided to persecute my daughters, so I tell the little shit that he is a little shit, which everybody knows, I raise my voice because I am French, and the mother flies to the rescue, all claws out, swashbuckling. I am carving the chicken so I wave emphatically a big kitchen knife, it seems to horrify her, she grabs her pestiferous offspring and takes him to her bedroom, locks the door. I can hear her trying to comfort the nefarious little louse, he's whining, sobbing, sputtering. After a few minutes she storms out, slams the door and leaves.

Everett decides to go to the fish market to see if they have fresh crabs.

Juli and I go down to the beach, we exchange a few words on what just happened, and we suddenly hear Sam-I-Am howling excruciatingly in the distance, like he was being skinned alive. We run up the stairs as fast as we can, Sheila comes from a different direction, haggard and dishevelled.

Lita is sitting on the windowsill picking her toes, placid and oblivious of the racket while Sam-I-Am is having a nervous breakdown in the broom closet where my two daughters have locked him in a touching display of solidarity. We heard later that he had accused little Claire of breaking the $2,000 real robot he got for Christmas and wanted to beat her up, so Gael, the older of my two princesses, took him by the scruff of the neck and threw him in the broom closet, while Claire was kicking him all the way for good measure.

The relationships between our two families are at their lowest, we can hardly look at each other. Sheila disappears once more in her bedroom to comfort her son, we hear him sob, then shriek: "I HATE THEM!" They did not come out for days, we only knew there was someone in that room because we saw Lita go back and forth laden with food, Champagne and toys. Good-natured Everett still perfunctorily tried to play the gracious host, but somehow lacked in the blissful liveliness that was his usual trademark. The New Year came and went, and we obscenely wallowed in our misery while bingeing on lobster, foie gras and caviar. A couple of hangovers finished us off, and eventually we did nothing, said nothing, went nowhere.

Meanwhile Lita, visibly encouraged by the misfortunes of her employers, was getting increasingly unpleasant and arrogant. Usually a specialist of passive resistance like many servants, she was openly refusing to follow directions or arguing endlessly when asked to do something. She slept in a recessed alcove adjoining her employers' bedroom, got up every day after Everett had made coffee, poured herself a cup and watched soap operas and videos on her little TV until dinner time. "It's our American permissiveness that's giving her ideas, I can't wait till we're back in Asia to get things straight", said Everett.

Three days before we were due to leave, Lita came to Juli in tears, begging for her help. Apparently, Sheila had completely lost her mind and accused Everett, in front of her, of "sleeping with the maid." Dumbstruck, Juli categorically refused to take sides in such a serious, sordid allegation, all the more so because we all knew that Sheila was a bit insane even if we always dismissed it with an amused shrug, and if there was something to be saved from the friendship, Juli was determined not to spoil it. Quite remarkably, it was soon Everett's turn to confide, in an uncharacteristic display of awkwardness and embarrassment: "I didn't know how to tell you, but Sheila seems to have gone completely out of control and I am really worried. She's always been a little bipolar, but her condition has gone seriously downhill, and all this drinking isn't helping. Now she's imagining things, she claims she heard conversations and witnessed events that never took place. I really don't know what to do, I'm at a loss."

We tried to be as comforting and conciliatory as we could to both while sitting on the fence, but we never missed an opportunity to reiterate the obvious: that Lita was extraordinarily unappealing, which seemed to sink in slowly and eventually make an impression on Sheila. This got us closer to her, and our last two days were almost bearable: we put on our best light-heartedness to pull Sheila out of her mental abyss and she made a commendable attempt at coming out for us, while Everett bounced back from his unexpected slump and regained some of his jovial persona. As for Lita, she stayed aloof and unnoticeable, looking more concave, yellowish and extinct than ever, but at least she stopped bickering or overacting. Our farewell, although relieving, was very sad, because we knew that it was the end of an era and the group would never meet again. We got all the more emotional.

****

Back home in Pittsburgh, Sheila told us almost jokingly after a few months that she had been diagnosed with a mild case of cirrhosis of the liver and had to give up Champagne, and that she had decided to renounce her marvellously androgynous, extra-small, vine-like dancer's body to have two big silicone blobs grafted on her chest. I was appalled.

"What's new? The American upper middle class again, their obsession with the bââââdy, and as always, that attraction to make-believes, forgeries, rubber noses, straightened teeth complete with whitening and polish, lasered body hair, skin pulled like a drum's and injected with botox… yuk!"

"No", Juli said, "you don't understand! She wants to please Everett, win him again on her own terms and come out a conqueror… She always resented being older, hated her small breasts, and the more Everett told her he loved them, the more she thought he was lying… She's going on large-scale manoeuvres to crush her own insecurities, she wants to own the high ground, dominate the battlefield…"

A case in point: on the spur of the moment, Sheila released her tempestuous Irishness on Lita and fired her again in a fit of rage, so even in her upbeat moments her insanity was reaching new heights. Juli found in that decision further proof of what she suspected: "See? She's getting rid of everything around her that has been, rightly or wrongly, a bone of contention, and more especially anyone who can show a semblance of femininity. She wants to reign supreme and uncontested."

I never gave it a second thought, just shrugged: "She's at it again!"

Then came a rather long, exuberant period, and everything had seemingly fallen into place: Sheila learned that she had been misdiagnosed so she started guzzling Roederer again with a vengeance, she apologized to Everett for falsely accusing him of being unfaithful at a time when she was really down in the dumps and her "judgment was clouded", and promptly called the maid back, Everett indulged in premeditated sensual explorations, and it looked like a new honeymoon was in the works. At last Sheila had overcome her curse, broken the downward spiral and the vicious circle of suspicion, depression and alcohol that was taking her to a mental state from which no recovery would be possible.

A few weeks later, I got a phone call from Everett. The couple had broken up, she threw him out of the house outright and had the locks changed.

"What happened? I thought you were swimming in bliss, spinning the perfect lovers' web…"

One evening, after they had dedicated themselves body, heart and soul to their renewed sexual eruptions, they were sipping their usual night cap and started a vaguely inebriated, tongue-and-cheek mental game on life as a couple – the little secrets each keeps from the other, and of course the necessity to disclose everything to create total trust. Everett agreed in principle, but argued that some truths could be hurtful, that no couple was ready to take all their skeletons out of their closets.

"No, no", Sheila said, "we are adults, we can take it, our couple is strong enough to withstand any such discoveries…"

Sheila only had very minor stuff on her conscience – more in the realm of intentions than actions, although she did put a powerful laxative in Lita's coffee once, just before she forced her to take the first plane back home. Conversely, she was firmly convinced that Everett could not keep a secret: she had noticed his smutty ogling each time Diditt was around and discovered the stash of stained magazines he was keeping in his secluded man-cave, which in a way she found rather reassuring because at least it indicated to her that he did not live out his fantasies in the arms of another woman. And lastly, she knew about his quirks, both from the very… "personal" arousing material he had had to bring to the fertility clinic, and from the XS French maid outfit branded *Wonder Lust* he was keeping in his walk-in closet, which she might even have been willing to wear for him, only he never dared to ask.

"Do you mean you have kept shameful things from me?" Everett asked.

"Well, like everyone else I suppose, a few embarrassing thoughts and deeds, but nothing very serious I hope, and you?"

"Me too!... Of course!"

"Let's have a test. You go first."

"No, you."

"Oh, come on, be a gentleman!"

"Are you sure you can take it?"

"I can take anything from you, my love."

"Sure? There will be no turning back, you know…"

"Go ahead, make my day."

"Last chance!"

"Oh, for God's sake!!!…"

"Ok then, here I go…"

A perfect gentleman, Everett bit the bullet.

He found himself barefoot on the doormat with a pair of spare underpants and a toothbrush in his hands and an acrid taste of wine in his mouth, while she was looking up her lawyer's number to ask for a divorce.

He had been schtupping the maid for eight years.

A Crease in the Cover
or
How I Became an Illiterate Writer

This was France, and we were locked in a time warp: between the end of the Algerian "peacekeeping operation" in 1962 and the 1968 riots, a world died but nobody knew.

Yet.

I was in school – as the expression went, "doing my humanities."

"Doing your humanities", in that dead world, meant that you were a good student, studious and… "dead serious", of course, and you were rewarded for your goodness by the much-coveted gift of Latin from grade 6 to grade 12. And if you were very good and very lucky, they even allowed you, from the 8th grade onwards, to study ancient Greek.

That dead world taught dead languages: a privilege, just like the one extended to those North African Harkis is who had been bestowed a violent, unceremonious death or, as the case may have been, a disgraced life in the pursuit of French peace.

"Doing your humanities" meant doing time.

Seven years of it. Like the Algerian war.

I was dying. We all were.

The French literature curriculum was simple and straightforward: the Middle Ages in the sixth grade, the sixteenth century in the seventh, seventeenth in the eighth, eighteenth in the ninth, nineteen in the tenth, twentieth in the eleventh.

And in the twelfth grade, no reprieve, Philosophy kicked in: 2,500 years of human thought memorized in ten months, at the rate of eight hours a week, by a cohort of unfinished, unpolished, unfulfilled teenagers whose heads were full of dates, quotations and antique verses.

As a crowning academic achievement, the prospect of a notoriously grueling exam at the end of high school and its inevitability loomed for years, getting more terrifying as it got closer. Not only were you doing time, you had to go through a thorough investigation, a guilt-ridden interrogation about things you should know, and a parole hearing all at once, or they put you back in bondage for another year.

Back to your boys' penitentiary.

Or your girls', but no mixing and no promiscuity: in that educational system, mutual ignorance was bliss, so peacekeeping could be smoothly implemented.

Those unfinished teenagers pondering the words of Descartes, Kant and Karl Marx and wisely debating wars, revolutions and the place of mankind in the universe had never seen a woman's tits.

But I did not complain, I was not unhappy, or not too much, maybe just stressed out: I had no idea of what a different world would be like, and besides I was among the privileged few, I was lucky, I even had financial aid! So I complied, I coped, I collaborated. I even excelled, and made it a point to outsmart my mortal enemy: the flat-footed child of a local politician, whom I managed to deprive, by collecting academic awards, of the laurel wreaths to which his submissiveness and his wondrous memorizing ability seemed to predispose him. I was never a Winston Smith, never idolized my torturers, but still: I took it all in, zealously and beyond the line of duty.

Well, almost all of it.

Literature was the stumbling block.

In the 6th grade, the brutal switch from the good-natured recitation of fables and telling of tales the year before to the processing of the medieval parlance and its interminable chants turned out to be quite daunting, and so was the passage from descriptive essays on grid paper to free-hand dissertations. I resisted, found solace in my old Belgian comics for a while, prolonged my childhood as much as I could, but it only got worse, the gap got wider. I who had never even read "The Little Prince", I never caught up, never could ease into Voltaire or Rousseau: as the appeal of being an eternal Peter Pan waned, the prospect of adulthood became increasingly horrifying, in a culture I saw as a huge, alien spaceship arbitrarily populated by ghosts in armors and top hats, with a few females in bodices. Meanwhile, the reader cannot begin to imagine what level of exasperation a whole generation got from people whose job it was to make us love literature. Thankfully, by the time I reached the 10th grade, I only had to briefly ponder my hatred of French romantics: near the end of the schoolyear, the whole country was in havoc and barricades were being erected in all major cities. Little wonder the May 1968 "events" started off in the ghetto of education, ignited by a trivial incident about regulations that prevented the nightly mingling of men and women on university campuses!

So by the time Hubert M… broke into my life with massive consequences, my perception of the literary landscape had evolved into a vast expanse of scorched earth from which emerged a few oases that my built-in flamethrower had missed or spared. The writers who escaped from the carnage included, for various reasons: Choderlos de Laclos, Rabelais, Molière, Victor Hugo, Marivaux, La Fontaine, Alphonse Daudet, Camus, Flaubert, and a few others. I wasn't a part of their worlds either, but they were powerful enough that I *wanted* to be.

And then, Hubert M... happened.

I did not know I was a fan of crime novels. Well... I hadn't read many crime novels, they weren't in the curriculum – maybe just a couple of Arsène Lupins, because they were only slightly matured extensions of Jules Verne's "Mysterious Island". After I had prolonged my childhood, I was trying to prolong my adolescence.

Then a schoolmate who was as lonely and distraught as I was brought me a book I *absolutely had to read* called "The Road to Hell", written by a former high school history teacher. I was a little flummoxed at first, since the last thing I wanted was to read a book written by a teacher, while the whole educational system was unsuccessfully attempting to make a reader of classics out of me. What clinched it was the title, which had the lure of damnation befitting my mental approach to literature, and it had consequently an appeal that even "Les Misérables" could not rival. At the time, I had not read Rimbaud or Baudelaire, and much less Edgar Allan Poe or H.P. Lovecraft. I took the book home, I still remember how shabby it looked, its dusty smell, its naïve, incomprehensible illustration of a pig between two window shutters, its worn-out paperback cover with one deep crease line in the bottom-right corner, and the unusual excitement I felt at rubbing it in my pocket.

The minute I opened the book, a genie came out. The only wish I made was the only wish he could not grant:

that the book never end. Everything else the book offered: a breathtaking plot, a flowery, highly sophisticated version of French so far unbeknownst to me, refinement, poetry, philosophy, humour, aesthetics, and the brilliant description of a world of unspeakable mediocrity dominated by women of superior intelligence and beauty. Being a great admirer of Laclos' *Dangerous Liaisons*, I was desperate for a more current version, and being a virgin, I could only imagine the quivering ballets and intimate ebulliences of those devilishly gorgeous creatures and I longed for them. I definitely wanted to be in *that* world.

Oh but the reader will certainly want to know more, about the plot, the ending... Well, it is a mystery novel, so by definition I cannot give away the punch line, disclose the final twist. All I can say is that it describes the arrival of a young teacher in a sleepy little French village where he just got his first posting. Everything seems peaceful and... normal, until he notices that some things are not *quite* right, he spots little details that make no sense: a teacher friend, his wife and their four children live in a tiny apartment they have to share with a gigantic Saint-Bernard, the bust of Socrates in the principal's office has rabbit's ears, the local priest is keeping a pig in the sacristy, and many other inexplicable oddities. In trying to find out why and connecting the dots as he gets to know the villagers better, he slowly uncovers stories of murder and rape, sex and blackmail, vices and perversions, compromised government and religious officials. Juicy stuff.

I don't remember exactly what triggered my immediate jubilation, I guess it was the whole package, the sudden suspicion that beyond the Gothic ramparts and moats of my school was another world, a rebellious reverse of the same culture – a dark web – outfitted with infra-red luminaries who would show me the way to pleasure, a realm that I yet had to discover. It was the arrogance, the insolence, the flamboyance, the anti-establishment bias that fed into a tone of brazen free-spiritedness which made it ever so exhilarating.

My first literary infatuation since the Smurfs.

I kept the book.

I am ashamed to admit that, much later, I began to realize, quite reluctantly at first, that Hubert M… may not have been that great a writer, but for now and the next couple of decades at least, I kept his cult alive and remained faithful to this puppy love, bought every new book he wrote and read it like the gospel, while vowing to stay true to the road to hell he had charted, and rejoicing in the fact that I had penetrated French literature from behind.

****

The immediate effect of this epiphany was that since real pleasure was not to be found in the mainstream, I had to search for it through the dark web of deplorable literature. This took me directly to the forbidden discovery of famous collaborationists of the Second World War, among whom Louis-Ferdinand Céline – who, at the time, was the most fashionable of black-listed, accursed writers, a genius plagued by his appalling antisemitism – and his nebula of right-wing anarchists. Then, I widened the circle, from the far right to the right, and then went on to real libertarians and humanists. I never really found much pleasure in the far left: too introspective, too caught up in questioning and unable or unwilling to give satisfactory responses, as in those days, the Soviet ideology clouded most of the thinking. This is how, through my process, Camus passed with flying colours, and Sartre mercilessly got an F. Céline and his revolutionary language introduced me to slang literature, with the delightful pulp fiction of the San-Antonio detective series, now considered unique and precious in literary history.

Another collateral effect of Hubert M...'s intervention was that, from then on, I expected a genie to come out of every book I endeavoured to read. This has not improved over the years, quite on the contrary: since I have less time left, I have none to lose, and I outright go for the jugular, I want instant gratification. I find it almost humiliating to have to go through half a book to find out whether I'm going to like it or not. Don't ask me to try and break into a writer's world, as I mostly expect that a writer will spontaneously and generously bring me into it. And if that writer has to grab me and rough me up a little, so be it: take me, I'm yours! I want a shock effect, thrills, love at first sight, a seismic experience. I expect nothing short of a miracle, and I believe in miracles, I know they exist because the Divine Hubert left the door forever ajar... The writers who could meet that impossible demand were few and far apart: there was Céline, of course, but apart from the Marquis de Sade, who blew my mind for a while, there were only isolated meteors, like Patrick Modiano, Christiane Rochefort, Panaït Istrati, Arthur Rimbaud, Jacques Prévert, Alexandre Vialatte, Kafka, Rezvani, Kazantsakis... Boris Vian provided some illumination and ushered me briefly into the world of pataphysics, but he was a flash in the pan. To reach total fulfillment again, I had to wait until I stumbled on Milan Kundera, who was the stylistic opposite of Hubert M... No frills, just bare irony underneath the apparent straightforwardness of simple words. His books were very short, increasingly so as he got older, and spoke volumes. But a lot of those authors were not even French any more. I was going further astray, never filled in the blanks, never looked back.

That drunken boat of mine continued its ruthless journey through a logic of its own, regardless of what treasures got stranded in its wake.

Then came the English tsunami, with a totally different feel to it. I had no moral responsibility towards English, it was not a language that demanded or claimed to be a part of me, so my approach to it was playful, gratuitous, hedonistic. While French was a kind of Jewish mother using guilt as a weapon, English appeared like a long-awaited, long-needed mistress, alluring, seductive, dedicated, giving, NSA, with the unrivalled aura conferred upon her by her illegitimate nature. I discovered with ravishment every fragrance, every texture her body was offering, I foraged into every scented hollow I saw, and since I am the kind of fellow who falls in love with his mistress, I tried to make her mine, knowing all the while that she was giving pleasure to millions of admirers. But I am not a jealous man. I can share. All I needed was to feel welcome and cherished, and I did.

I still do.

After a brief introduction through British writers such as Coleridge, William Golding, George Orwell, D.H. Lawrence and the Liverpool poets of the 70s, Henry Miller was my first real object of veneration, and then I went on to William Burroughs, William Styron, Ken Kesey, Philip Roth, Ray Bradbury, Isaac Asimov, Thomas Scott, and without any sense of propriety or prioritization, any compromise with snobbishness or what I would call "fashionability", the three pulp fiction superstars Stephen King, John Grisham and Michael Crichton. I can't say movies were not instrumental in such discoveries. Both art forms were interconnected, movies leading to literature and literature to movies. My Jewish mother and my mistress almost fell into each other's arms in 1988-1989, when Milos Forman and Stephen Frears, almost simultaneously, made two very different but equally magnificent movie versions of one of my favourite books: "Dangerous liaisons". Interestingly, the first-ever movie version had been made by Roger Vadim, Brigitte Bardot's first husband. In it, writer/musician/pataphysician Boris Vian played one of his only four movie roles. An almost perfect closing of the loop.

Was Nabokov, that multi-lingual Russian aristocrat, an English or a French writer? All I know is that "Lolita" gave me one of my life's greatest pleasures, in both languages, and the Kubrick movie offered a lot more than icing on the cake. It introduced a new dimension by depicting the inner world of an Englishman living in the United States who gets fooled by the very language he thinks he owns, unaware that its local connotations elude him completely. A monument of double entendre, with a perversity that was even superior to my ambiguous relationship with two different languages.

It was the best of times, it was the worst of times, and the worst was on the French side. I was living in a state of permanent guilt for abandoning my mother to go live an unstructured, lurid life in English-speaking countries, and the now fashionable "fear of missing out" was my way of life. This has not stopped. When I was 20 years old, I decided that since the work of Marcel Proust was the subject of such high praise, there must be something to it, so I bought *Swann's Way* with the firm intention of giving it a fair chance. A week later, I put the book down, at page 67 – I remember because I tried to pick it up again several times in the weeks that followed, only to lose heart and stumble repeatedly on that ill-fated number. Forty years went by. By then, I had talked myself into believing that the cause of my dislike four decades earlier had simply been that I was too young and not mature enough to appreciate it, so I purchased the book again. After a week labouring over the literary implications of the totally unnecessary opening sentence that became a standard feature of the most learned treatises: "For a long time, I went to bed early", I actually went to sleep. For the second time in many years, I had put the book down. The other day, I came across the book again, and it opened extempore... on page 67. Of course, it was a different time, a different layout and a different publisher, but still, I thought I saw a sign in that random episode.

****

My life as a traitor, an impostor and a double agent reached a triumphant if nefarious peak when the government of France made me a proposal I could not refuse. By a twist of fate – and probably also because my total lack of a moral fiber, after François Mitterrand was elected, had caused me to opportunistically pretend to be a socialist (or rather forget to say I was not) – I was offered a foreign posting in Toronto, as the director of a cultural center. They might as well have handed over the directorship of an opera to a deaf man. I was supposed to lead an orchestra when all I could do was read lips.

Among other things, I was in charge of... literary events.

This was fifteen years after my discovery of Hubert M... By then, I had gotten a Masters' degree in Anglo-American studies, spent one year in England and seven years in New York, most of my friends were English-speakers and so was my wife, my betrayal of French had been duly consummated and I was in the throes of becoming a renegade. Because of its more-than-comfortable remuneration, however, that job convinced me not to turn into an outright deserter and wait a while, so I became the next most contemptible thing: a mercenary. I was young, my infamy was boundless, and I was well on my way to repudiating my own mother.

But this was not to be.

I just teetered at the edge of the abyss, enjoyed the inebriation, felt some exhilaration gazing into the vacuum.

Eventually, I was saved from perdition.

By Hubert M...

For fifteen years I had followed his progress, from one mystery masterpiece to the next, one award after another, then on to historical sagas, movies, TV appearances, food reviews. Every now and then I would pick up *The Road to Hell* in my hands, read a random passage, make a few annotations on those useless blank pages at the back of the book, smell its dusty scent, run my fingers along the deep crease on the cover. Hubert M... was the strongest link I kept with French literature – and reassuringly so, because I only had to open one of his books to stop wondering why.

I had been at my job for a couple of years, unknowingly witnessing the slow coming of age of a sprawling city which seemed to have been built in the countryside and wondering about my place in it, when a life-changing piece of news landed on my desk in a brown envelope. Among a tentative list of French lecturers to be used as pillars of my cultural programming was the name of Hubert M...And I had the power to invite him or turn him down!

I did not turn him down.

I was in my thirties, curbing my enthusiasm for all things great and small, and painfully discovering disappointment and cynicism, so I was mindful that our first contact might prove unsatisfactory, and I tried to work myself up to it. I knew and feared that Hubert M...'s stellar artistry might conceal a heinous disposition: after all, Céline was an appalling, pitiful anti-Semite and Picasso himself displayed sadistic cruelty with women.

The man I picked up at the airport was every bit what I expected, only worse. What comes to my mind when I try to recall our only encounter are two of my most cherished, albeit quite detestable, English words: "supercilious" and "curmudgeon". To complicate things even further, this virtuoso of the French language had the physique of a lumberjack, which completely detracted from the kind of impact his writing created and gave me a rather uneasy feeling, so communication was awkward, even unpleasant at times. But to remain within the league of rarely spoken words, I might add, much to his credit, that his lecture caused quite a kerfuffle in the well-wishing world of conventional bookworms.

He had style. Loads of it.

He gave a brilliantly erudite, stylish, thought-challenging lecture, and my enthusiasm was instantly rekindled. Then came question period, and as usual, the foolish inquiry: "How did you become a writer?" This is, from memory, what he replied.

"I married a very beautiful wife. Beautiful women have entitlements, and since beauty itself is perceived as an entitlement by the beautiful, I had to face a two-tiered process that was unobjectionable and quite impossible to by-pass or overcome – or at least, not if I wanted to retain the cannibalistic pleasures attached to the appropriation, exploration and gentle invasion of beauty. And as poet Jacques Prévert had one of his characters say in the cinematic masterpiece *Children of Paradise*: 'beauty is an exception, an insult to the world that's ugly.' In full awareness of my own unsightly appearance, I considered myself hugely lucky for my enslavement and dependency. One entitlement of beautiful women, to our utmost satisfaction, is quite simply that their beauty be kept and made perennial. This triggers a visual maintenance and enhancement process which in turn entails the purchase of costly trinkets. Their skin texture must be constantly softened and smoothed out by the most luxurious ointments, and since you cannot have a beautiful woman leave anything in her trail but a luscious fragrance, you are sentenced to walk around over-lit glass-and-chrome boutiques with coffee beans in one hand and a credit card in the other.

'A beautiful woman is expensive. I had to find money.

'As a history teacher, I could barely treat a lady to a movie and nibbles, so it became clear to me that our precarious love was bound to dissolve in dishwater if I did not take drastic action.

'What can a man do when he has no other skill than the regurgitation and hammering out of dates and events to a – literally – captive audience longingly looking through the window at the chestnut trees in the playground? Being quite verbose by nature, the one thing I had always found relatively easy was write, so why not?

'The next thing was to decide what literary genre I was going to mass-produce. It seemed to me that the most popular form of pulp fiction would be conducive to the juiciest income, so I chose crime novels.

'And there you have it. My only lucky break was to find a publisher. And I'm not even sure he liked me that much. Maybe he just wanted to shut me up.

'Satisfied?"

The audience was speechless.

Of course, he could only be iconoclastic and self-deprecatory because he was successful, but I still was young enough to take his word for it, so I fully adhered to a new, unceremonious, down-to-earth view of literature. After all, it was just a secretion of the mind, like any talent in any field, like the body secretes urine. I could do it, anybody could do it, or do something else.

We finished the evening in an upscale local restaurant, where Hubert M... displayed the full extent of his culinary knowledge and expertise. By the end of the evening, I think that his obvious initial dislike of me had turned into mild appreciation, and my love into worship.

It was a whirlwind tour, and he was gone the next day.

****

My French friend Maurice had come all the way from Ottawa to watch his new literary idol perform, and he joined us for dinner. In the gallery of misfits that flocked around my operatic life at the time, if I was the deaf orchestra leader, Maurice was the barytone-turned-castrato. He too had the physique of a lumberjack, which seemed to predispose him to a life of ruggedness and dirty jokes, only he was gay, refined, dainty and fastidious.

And quite lovable.

From under the coarse hair that covered the back of his hands and fingers emerged impeccably manicured nails, and from below his thick moustache came the most antiquated, precious, quaint *vieille France* words, uttered in a gravelly but strangely effeminate tone. He belonged to the older generation of gays, with one foot in the closet and one foot outside, who did not quite know what kind of person they wanted to be or could be, and who craved for friendship.

I was his friend.

He had style too, and he loved Hubert M...

It was he who initiated the next episode of the Hubert M... saga.

****

Maurice had discovered Hubert M... through *The Virgin*, a best-selling historical novel about Joan of Arc's trial. It was Hubert M...'s first real foray into a higher form of literature mixing historical fiction and documentary. Although the master excelled in it, he "only" wrote about a dozen of books in that genre over the years. I suspect that the amount of research and inevitable inflation of words, footnotes, explanatory passages descriptive of past lifestyles made it a very lengthy, laborious process where stylistic purity and consistency were difficult to maintain. In my view, and that is my only reservation, he never found the ideal balance between the vain, narcissistic and sometimes gratuitous temptation for an erudite to display outright erudition, and the necessity for a sustained, vigorous plot whose twists and turns would preserve without dilution the reader's eagerness and anticipation. In any case, he always ended up back to square one, repenting to have neglected what he affectionately called his "pot-boilers", and turning them out like hot cakes, with a vengeance.

Maurice had read Hubert M...'s "noble" literature first, but he was so enthralled by his discovery that he looked far and wide to find other work that the writer had done. So naturally he started off with the first mystery novel the author ever wrote – a story of sex, money, conspiracy, cruelty and murder called *The Praying Mantises*, which brought its creator sudden recognition and a major award at the age of thirty-two. Like me, like the jury for the Grand Prize of Crime Fiction, Maurice was an instant fan.

A late bloomer, Maurice had two of Hubert M…'s books. I had twelve.

Maurice stayed at my place for a few days after the lecture. One evening, while we were liberally dousing our snouts with Cognac after savouring a delicious venison roast and wild boar sausages, Maurice forcefully expressed his hatred of hunting.

"Hunting was my father's passion, he loved its culture of manliness, its masonic-like traditions and quite simply its primeval violence, and for years he took me with him – never came to terms with a son who would burst into tears at the sight of a dead animal, though. I wanted no part in it. I still don't. I was a great disappointment to my father".

"I'll bet".

"But I do love game meats and I eat my steaks blue. Hypocrisy? Not really. Some things just have to stay unspoken, masqueraded or simply rephrased to spare our newly acquired, 'civilized' squeamishness. The invaluable ambergris used in the manufacturing of so many exquisite perfumes is just whale poop, foie gras is a form of cirrhosis of the liver induced in ducks and geese, lobsters are given the Joan of Arc treatment before we playfully put on our funny bibs, and black pudding is a euphemism for blood sausage. As usual, don't ask, don't tell, this is the price for peace. And I never tried to see signs in tea leaves, but maybe, through my sudden discovery of Hubert M…, my father is sending me from beyond the grave the go-ahead to exorcise him…"

"How so?"

"Who's the patron saint of hunters?"

"St. Hubert."

"Exactly."

I guess I was touched by this evocation. When Maurice left my house, he had in his luggage eight of my most beloved books, that he promised he would mail back to me as soon as he had read them. Before I parted from *The Road to Hell*, I closed my eyes and, in a gesture that had become half-pagan fetishism, half-religious rite, I ran my fingers along the deep crease in the cover.

****

The years went by. Naturally, Maurice never returned my books. I would sometimes ask and he'd answer maliciously: "They're in the mail." It became obvious to me that I would never see those novels again – not in his lifetime. Maurice and I remained friends; we just avoided the topic, and I think I even managed to forget. And in my few moments of clear thinking, I even found a moral to the whole story: after all, I had stolen *The Road to Hell*, and it was only fair that I be punished for it.

Three years after Hubert M...'s lecture, I made a few months' stopover in France, and went on to take a new posting in Singapore. Meanwhile, Maurice's stint in Ottawa came to an end and he moved back to a small apartment he had in Paris. I did not hear from him in over a year.

Then came a devastating announcement, from Maurice's mother: Maurice had passed away, taken from us, as I learned later, by that abominable disease that claimed the lives of so many of our gentlest, most cultured and often most humorous friends. I was beyond inconsolable.

On my next trip to Paris, I went to pay my respects. The old lady still showed unspeakable grief at reminiscing the life of her only child and I tried to comfort her as much as I could, but I ended up pitifully sharing her pain and probably worsening it.

And then…

Out of the corner of my eye, on a shelf, neatly arranged and displayed, were…

My books!

She must have noticed the direction of my glance, because she said without looking: "You can have them back. I know they're yours, Maurice told me." And although I would have given all my valuables plus my right arm to see Maurice's ruddy face come through the door again, I clumsily, shamefully took the books, penetrated by the crushing, yet disarmingly uplifting knowledge that one of that dying man's last thoughts had been for me.

****

Back to my hotel, I unpacked the books, and… there were seven!

Not eight, seven!

I looked repeatedly into my briefcase, turned it upside down, inside out, but one book had definitely vanished. I just hoped it was not…

Yes, it was!… *The Road to Hell* was missing.

What was I going to do? To go back to a heartbroken mother and rummage through her deceased son's personal things was out of the question, so I headed for the Gibert bookstore on Boulevard St. Michel to see if I could buy a new copy.

"Out of print."

"For how long?"

"Years."

"Is a reprint due soon?"

"Dunno."

More years went by. Every time I got near a French bookstore I would go in, check it out, and the response was always the same.

"Out of print."

The Internet came along, and it became easier to get the latest updates.

The latest updates were the same as the earlier updates.

"Out of print."

The matter was beyond technology.

One day, I went back to the Gibert bookstore and one of the employees made an unexpected suggestion: "Why don't you go to our second-hand outlet, right across the street? Maybe they will have a used copy."

The section devoted to mystery stories, crime novels and other forms of inferior literature was on the highest floor, right under the roof of the building. There was only one lone customer browsing through the shelves, an older, nondescript gentleman who could have been a ghost; behind a desk sat a 27 or 28-year-old girl wearing thick horn-rimmed glasses, sexy in an intellectual, slightly smug way.

"Do you know Hubert M...?"

"'Course."

"Do you have any of his books?"

"Only one. They're not the kind of books people buy and sell. No value, you see, they belong more in a yard sale."

"Which one?"

"I believe it's called 'The Road to Hell'. Very good book, you'll like it."

My heart leapt in my chest, my voice started trembling.

"Can I take a look?"

"Please yourself. It's right there on the highest shelf and I can't reach. You can use the step ladder."

I went up two steps, and when I picked up the familiar paperback, I almost fell off my perch.

On the bottom right of the front cover, my hand felt a deep crease.

****

How my own book ended up in the attic of a second-hand bookstore beats me, it is a mystery that will probably never be solved. But what I know is that shortly thereafter, I developed an urge to memorialize the magic of life, of which I had been a prime witness. Was Maurice giving me from beyond the grave the go-ahead to write books of my own? I do not usually look for signs in tea leaves either, but it certainly was a moment in my life when things started coming together.

But slowly. Ever so slowly. So slowly it is only with the passing of time that I can find a pattern.

My father had died a few years before, in my arms on the platform of a railroad station, and I wanted to write a page strictly for myself, to express and remember the complexity and intensity of my feelings. That one page took twelve years to write: twelve years of soul-searching, twelve years trying to find the right words. Then the floodgates opened and I wrote 300 pages in six months. That was my first book. I have written seven. All in French.

One year, on a sudden flash of inspiration, I set out to write a novel about a girl whose sexuality was developing and who saw it as an orchid growing inside her, then gradually taking over. It turned out to be an unusually easy task, the book practically wrote itself. I called it *L'Orchidiable* ("The Orchidevil"). Only years later was it brought to my attention that the name of one of Hubert M...'s early, lesser-known novels was *Le Cupidiable*

("The Cupidevil"). Did that one book mysteriously fall through the cracks? Did I subliminally single out and register that title from a random list of Hubert M...'s books, just to regurgitate and process it decades later? Maybe.

At some point also, I got rid of my mental clutter and came to terms with who I really was – when I realized that the choice of a language over another, of a culture over another, of my mother or my mistress, was not an inevitability, that I could have both and one would not detract from the other. It simply could not be put in mathematical terms: my adoption of English has not made me less of a Frenchman. I am 100% French. But I am *also something else*. The language issue has always been an identity issue, but writing has the merit of clarifying some of it. Gustave Flaubert said: "I am Madame Bovary." In that sense, I am both the Eiffel Tower and McDonald's, I am every experience, every sensitivity I decide to own.

In the process, I never filled in the blanks, and my cultural gaps only widened. More than ever, I am an illiterate writer. I romanticized it by proudly stating it was caused by my initial revolt against the system and my rejection of it, but it may just have been laziness, only I'm good at self-complacency.

I'll live with it. It has not prevented me from discovering the genius of Albert Cohen, so it's all good.

Lately, I have taken to writing in English. Why? Probably because writing in French, for me, is similar to what Groucho Marx called "being a Jew comedian" was for him. It is expected. And it bores me. The road to hell, of which I helped pave a reasonable portion, starts off with a sign saying: "No expectations please."

Let's see where it takes me.

Hubert M... passed away three years ago, at the age of ninety. Just in time to see a remarkable movie version of one of his masterpieces, *Return from the Ashes*. The name is *Phoenix*, and it is a German movie.

Those are all the thoughts that go through my mind when I rub my fingers against the deep crease on the cover of what used to be my favourite book.

A genie still comes out.

How Things Got Like This

Where I'm bound, I can't tell
-Bob Dylan

The pretty hooker across the street is waving at him, bare breasted at her window. She complains about the heat, then laughs in a clear, youthful voice. It is nighttime and no-one is sleeping on West 48th Street, just making small talk.

Laurent lives in a tiny three-story walk-up. He too keeps his window open but leaves his air-conditioning unit on, winter and summer, to cover the noise from the street. When he goes to bed, he has to shut the blinds or the flickering neon sign next to the brothel keeps him awake. He is in a *film noir*, Humphrey Bogart on the run. He loves the feeling.

He had been warned to choose his neighborhood very carefully, down to the street or even the building, but when he landed here, he only saw an alien architecture streaked with the zigzags of fire escapes, and endlessly wandered through multicoloured, unidentifiable Martian crowds. All his reference points became unreadable and a persistent case of jetlag made it all unimportant anyway, so he picked the first apartment he could find, all in a blur. The movie on Air France was *The Man Who Would be King*, but he did not hear the dialogue because he had never taken a plane before and was too intimidated to ask for headphones.

This is not the New York of the 21st century, where the devil will wear Prada in his own Kitchen, but of *Midnight Cowboy* and *Taxi Driver* – grimy, gritty, bankrupt, festering in a murky zone on the edge of sanity. The theatres look glitzy and the streets are pervaded by the scent of food, but those façades, those restaurants have a bedlam of misery, disease and trafficking huddled at their doors, barely contained by a scattered deployment of howling sirens and overweight shadows in blue uniforms.

Here, right at the cusp of Times Square and Hell's Kitchen, the world is spreading thin.

****

How he managed to convince *Le Journal du Midi* to appoint him as their special correspondent in the US remains a mystery, even for him. Of course, "special correspondent", a pompous figure of speech, only referred to a glorified free-lancer pushing paper from one unreliable payment to the next, but it was an election year and the bicentennial of the American revolution was looming, so something huge was bound to happen – at least that was the case he made with great eloquence and passion to the senior editor. The Vietnam war had just ended and President Gerald Ford, when alerted to the unfathomable abyss in which Mayor Abraham Beame had plunged his city, allegedly urged New York to "drop dead". Indeed, something huge was brewing, and Martin Scorsese, albeit fictionally, had just earmarked New York as the metaphoric epicenter of a probable Armageddon. Nothing sells better than sin and the promise of eternal damnation.

He had read *Tintin in America*, so he thought he was fully equipped.

******

In the next building, up a few stairs, is a rickety awning with a sign saying *Restaurant Le Carnac*, and directly across, at street level, is *Pierre au Tunnel*. The owner of the first one is from Brittany, the other's from the Pyrenees, the two regions which regularly outdo each other as the poorest in France. Laurent pushed the door of *Le Carnac* a few times in the evenings and was invariably taken aback by the oddity of the place. While a few scattered customers were munching unconvincingly on a steak-frites or a croque-madame, three or four shadowy figures were sitting at the bar, drawn, with a thick, graphite stubble on their chins and eyes the color of charcoal. They spoke French – or a distant brand of it, punctuated with yeahs, wells and you-knows. They all had landed In New York thirty years before, except for a frail elderly gentleman they called *Monsieur Morganti* who would only show up occasionally and had immigrated at the end of the Great War. He never worked in restaurants, but on the harbour, on the waterfront, and in factories when industry was booming. *I could have been a contender* was a regret he never had because that in itself would have been a luxury, a state of mind he never contemplated, and neither did they. None of them had graduated to the suburbs, none of them had made it out of the city, just to some interzones in Brooklyn and Queens. None of them had kept any other connection to France than each other. Most of the time, they were drinking Ricard quietly, but every now and then, quite unexpectedly and for no apparent reason, they would suddenly stand up all at once, get a table and play cards, oblivious of propriety or legality. No *maître d'* in that setup, and since they never ate anything, no waiter either. The waiters knew. The bartender knew. When Laurent introduced himself, they were polite but reserved, showed no particular interest, asked no questions. They were curious about nothing, surprised by nothing. They were like ancient reefs that only briefly emerge from the mud when the tide is at its lowest.

They never invited him to play cards.

But what does it matter now?

There is an empty building a couple of blocks away, soon to be torn down. It is a cube with broken windows in the middle of a vacant lot, standing like a decaying molar fifteen storeys high. There are no signs, on the façade or elsewhere, not a single hint of what it might have been. The people at *Le Carnac* use it as a landmark, a kind of beacon, to find their way around. They call it casually the "French hospital", nobody knows why or nobody wants to tell. In Hells' Kitchen, those are the only items reminiscent of anything French: a few dusty awnings, a few jagged reefs barely outcropping as the waves of change get heavier, and an empty name, virtually just a figure of speech.

Laurent hesitates for a second. Which way should he go, right or left? On the left is Eighth Avenue. Monsieur Morganti told him that a couple of years ago they found a corpse cut up in pieces in a garbage can at the street corner, but urban legends are rampant in the world's second largest city. Eighth Avenue is all peep shows, sex shops and adult video stores, and the local movie theatre has been offering "Deep Throat" and "The Devil in Miss Jones" as a double feature for years, besieged by a clique of hustlers, pushers, dealers, tramps, streetwalkers. This is the time when theatres let their audiences out and restaurants go through another peak hour, and he doesn't feel like squeezing through the crowd with his hand on his wallet, twisting his neck into a 360-degree rotation like an owl to spot where trouble might come from. But mostly, he wants to avoid the Ritz, he doesn't want to be anywhere near a place that would remind him of where they met.

Ninth Avenue, only a couple of hundred yards away, is another world, and Laurent decides to head there for lack of a better option. He walks past the Belvedere Hotel, where heart-rending screams, always a woman's, are regularly heard between two gargoyles in the sky. Nobody seems to take any notice of it, the police never come. The art deco cachet of the hotel could make it a landmark, but the first signs of dereliction have appeared, the paint is peeling off and black mold is starting to show in the lobby and in the rooms. He interviewed a French rock musician there once, and when he arrived the musician was in bed smoking, probably thinking he was John Lennon. Laurent could not concentrate, had all his attention focused on the top of the headboard, where dozens of cockroaches kept marching in single file. His paper was bought by *Le Journal* anyway, but he made up most of it.

Fleur wouldn't be caught dead in a place like this, he thinks, and it brings a smile to his face.

He was told to avoid Ninth Avenue like the plague, because for uptowners *it was* the plague, the first installment of Spanish Harlem, unspeakably violent and racist. But he liked it right away. Sure, it was a Puerto Rican hub and every store front seemed to blare out Salsa music, but there were delivery trucks, greengrocers, hardware stores... Working men were walking the streets in decent attire, and proper ladies were holding the hands of little girls in white socks and patent-leather Mary Janes on their way to church on Sundays. Sure, the neighbourhood was a far cry from scenic, but singer Celia Cruz, although the picture of ugliness herself, knew how to shimmy irresistibly to Cuban music like no-one, with a liveliness and a grace of her own. Sure, it was poor, but it was dignified. And there were no drugs, the Irish mafia would not allow it.

For this was still the turf of the Irish mafia. The latest influx of population, the Hispanic one, had left umpteen pockets from previous settlements virtually untouched: Italian delis, Jewish tailors, Greek ice cream parlours, but most notably a network of pubs and various social establishments through which the Irish perpetuated their hold on illicit activities West of 8th Avenue. The Spillanes ran the mob from their headquarters at The White House bar, and the McManuses held sway on the political arena from the Midtown Democratic Club: this was the way the Irish kept the peace. And if one druggie crossed the invisible border between Times Square and Hell's Kitchen, Eddie "The Butcher" Cummiskey and his gang would make sure that his body was cremated for free – albeit anonymously – in a well-known incinerator by the docks that smelled of pulled pork. This did not prevent Mickey Spillane from visiting sick residents and giving out free turkeys to the poor on Thanksgiving.

On Ninth Avenue, there is a place called "Los Amigos", where Laurent often goes for a late-night snack. The owners are Chinese from Cuba, but they speak a brand of Chinese no Chinaman would understand and their Spanish borders on the surrealistic. Still, no English here: the left side of their menu is in Chinese, the right side in Spanish, and there is no evidence that one is a translation of the other. For some reason, they have taken a liking to Laurent, and since he is always writing something, they call him *escritor*: the scribe. They bring him his *mondongo* – a tripe and pigs' feet soup – without him even asking, and as he eats it, they invariably pause to look at him, laugh and make comments, they can't believe that a white guy should like that kind of stuff! He never has the heart to turn it down, always gives them a thumbs-up, he would hate to disappoint.

And further down towards 42nd Street is Bruno's, which makes the best manicotti in town. Even Fleur asked him to bring her some once.

****

He met Fleur at the New York Ritz, a new monument to the hubris of property developers determined to gentrify Times Square, built right next door to Show World, its 20,000 square feet of live sex acts and its 100 "showgirls". He liked to relax and decompress there when he was sick of the squalor of 8th Avenue and the sheer poverty of 9th and wanted to get a carefree, uplifting feeling of affluence and laid-back sophistication. Surprisingly, *Leo's*, a luxury pub with wood paneling, brass fixtures and a rooftop terrace, was not that expensive, and from Happy Hour to closing time it drew a reassuring crowd of journalists from the nearby offices of the *New York Times*, a number of silver foxes, many beautiful women, some obnoxious producers and showbiz show-offs, and occasionally the odd Broadway celebrity. He never took anyone there, whether friend or foe. This public place was an invaluable part of his private world, an observation platform, a voyeur's paradise – his own man-cave, custom-made to fit the scope, the scale and the soul of New York.

Then Fleur came.

She was sitting at the bar, idle and bored in front of a huge dry martini, stabbing the olives repeatedly with the miniature plastic sword that came with the drink and its two green Manzanillas, obviously waiting for something.

Or someone.

Unfortunately, as he found out, it was someone. Had it been something, he might have had a chance, he thought. Anybody might have had a chance.

At the precise moment when he caught a glimpse of her in the crowd, the bar went completely quiet for a millisecond and the world froze, or at least that is the way he wants to remember her first appearance – but he did hold his breath and his heart missed a beat. Perfectly matching the shiny redness of her lips, she was wearing a short dress draping her skillfully from a single clasp on her shoulder, of a textured and slightly shiny fabric like shantung or dupion, with a cleavage which was modest but evocative, and on her feet a pair of classic black pumps. Her whole presence was infused with a discreet but noticeable elegance, a touch disconnected, just a little too dressy for cocktail hour, yet without the formal harnessing of evening wear. She had a slightly exotic look, with high cheekbones and big almond-shaped eyes set wide apart, and her skin, although fair, had the special warmth and golden quality of fresh bread, its soft luster beautifully enhanced by a hint of rouge. Her features were quite stunning, and he marveled at the sweet roundness of her chin and the harmonious alignment and proportions of her nose, which were of rare artistry and delicacy. She had put her shiny black hair up, and Laurent could peek between two gesticulating customers at the unusual length of her neck and the undulating oval of her ear, adorned with a single pearl like an oyster. A lone strand of hair had escaped from the tightness of her bun, and she was routinely trying to push it back in, like she had probably done dozens of times before, unaware of her own grace or totally unconcerned by it. The potent effect of this furtive foray into the intimacy of her boudoir manners bewildered him.

Then a figure with grey hair appeared from nowhere, took her by the arm and pulled her away. "Put it on my tab", he heard the gravelly voice say.

Laurent had only had a vision of this intensity, experienced that kind of dazzlement once before, when he was a student – a fleeting encounter, a non-event on a Paris suburban train. No splendour there, just faded, huddled silhouettes while an early morning drizzle was spraying the car windows in gusts. Why that girl stood out so powerfully mystified him, but there was *something* about her, a sense of brightness and sweet surrender that split the dreariness of the commuting hour like a laser beam. He had miraculously found a seat diagonally across from her, avoided her glance yet could not help looking himself, pretending to be grave and lost in his thoughts – he was so young then! When their eyes connected, she gave him a pleasant smile, almost intimate, as though they had known each other a long time, at least it was his interpretation. When Laurent reluctantly got up to leave, she made a strange gesture with her hand, as though she wanted him to stay. With the passing of time, he does not remember whether that sign was even intended for him.

Laurent always hated himself for freezing at that special moment, for his inertia, his failure to tug on that tear in the fabric of normalcy and stretch it as long and wide as he could. For months he tried to find her, kept taking the same train back and forth, ate, slept, studied in cars that were packed with nondescript crowds or strewn with loose pages of *Le Parisien*, unfinished crossword puzzles and empty lunch bags, changed the time slot constantly. He did not know where she got on and off on that day, but he went all the way to the end of the line, desperately trying to believe in miracles and ready to take punishment for it.

He took the punishment.
He never saw her again.
And now that girl in the bar…

****

Laurent stops for a minute in front of 46th Street, wonders if he should make a left on Restaurant Row, but the street itself is exhaustingly touristy and uninteresting, and it would take him back to 8th Avenue, Times Square, Leo's, Tad's steak house and all things Fleur. Of course, he could force himself to think of something else until he hit a wealthier, more respectable area where he could shake away his blues and immerse himself in something else, Art Deco for instance – an over lit Rockefeller Center or a scintillating Radio City Music Hall would do the trick. In passing, he would walk along 47th Street, visit again the stretch of the diamond district where they shot that scene of *Marathon Man* which has Laurence Olivier recognized as the infamous Nazi doctor Christian Szell by an old lady who survived the holocaust… but it's getting very late, diamonds are back in their drawers, displays are covered in inconspicuous unbleached fabric and yarmulkes are all put away for the night, all the way to Williamsburg.

So he heads for 42nd Street and Port Authority, will go one last time through that parking lot where everybody gets mugged. He will take the A train to the Village, which seems like the only reasonably upbeat thing to do. And on second thoughts, never mind if it reminds him of Fleur, he knows everything will anyway.

****

For a couple of weeks he went back to Leo's, almost every night, sat at the bar and spent his stipends on double dry Martinis. He tried not to get too obsessional about Fleur, desperately wanted to exorcise his Parisian experience. But he still went. Nick the chubby sixty-year-old who was running the bar seemed to take a liking to him, would make enough elixir at the bottom of the shaker to serve him an extra shot with a wink. It was a little watered down, but who cared? Laurent's visits had become like a kind of pilgrimage, a trip to Lourdes hoping for a miracle that would cure his crippled mind, and he even had the holy firewater to drown his sins in.

And then, one day, she came back.

She sat at one end of the bar, alone, ordered a dry Martini, like most everybody did. She wore different clothes, but still in her own palette, a highly vivid, uncompromising combination of red and black. Laurent, who was always seeking a state of grace in inebriation, sobered up instantly. He wanted to go to her, tell her about Paris, about life and the dazzlement of love, even came up with the crazy thought that maybe he would kneel in public, work the crowd for her, ask for their endorsement and let his heart regurgitate all the poetry that was choking him, surely she wouldn't ridicule him in front of everybody, would she? And who cared what they might think anyway? He tried to slide off his stool elegantly but his knees buckled. His ankle gave out, he almost fell, let out a faint moan and managed to pull himself back up.

By the time he regained his composure, her bun was already bobbing up and down in the crowd, heading for the exit. From what he could see, she was with a man. A different one.

Never once did she look his way, he thought.

Another few weeks passed. He lost all hope of seeing her again and thought nothing of it: after all, he had already squeezed three unlucky strikes out of life so he was definitely out, those were the rules of miracle hunting and any other possibility was unimaginable. He was just back to normal, to a mindset he should never have been such a fool to even dream of changing. Beauty didn't want him, had no use for him, didn't even see him. Beauty wanted to curl up and shrivel in the arms of men who had lived too long to be willing or able to pay it the tribute it deserved, who didn't *feel* it like he did and only used it as a badge, an insignium, a toy, the gift of a red firetruck to which an eternal little boy eternally spoiled was eternally entitled. But still, Leo's had become a habit to him, the center of the world like Perpignan's railroad station was to Salvador Dali, he would use the place as his headquarters and seek inspiration in bar fumes and noisy after-work babble to scribble his columns. One evening, at a public phone at the end of the hall, he was trying to dictate a paper on the serial killer they called "the Son of Sam" to a Parisian contact who evidently resented being woken up in the middle of the night. A shadow brushed past him, leaving a faint, almost fruity scent of mock orange in its wake, and he knew that it was her.

"You and I should have a fling", she murmured.

****

Some subway stations are like the city square in front of a medieval cathedral, and 42nd Street is one of them. There are beggars, magicians, pickpockets, entertainers, acrobats, dancers, jugglers, hunchbacks…. It is the revenge of the street, of the people. The ghetto, its pent-up anger and its teeming life have gone overboard, all that bubbling brown sugar is now spilling out on the sidewalks of the self-righteous, using every underground passage, seeping through every chink in their armour. A mere five or six years before, the first community murals appeared, then hip-hop and breakdance, in some of the most destitute areas of the city, those that were beyond salvation: the Bronx, Harlem, the Lower East Side. And they spread like wildfire.

The A train suddenly bursts full speed into the station, hellishly noisy and painted up with enormous, gaudy designs. The renaissance of the Inner City has attracted the graffiti culture, and New York has become its new center. In Philadelphia, it was a misdemeanour. In New York, it has become an art form, complete with graphic styles and codes, unwritten rules, protocol, etiquette, contests for the highest bridges to smear, the loftiest towers to daub, and a lingo of its own that talks about throw-ups, bubble style, tags, burners… An angry new form of music, a cascade of imprecations with a beat called "rap", is the anthem of the new nation.

The train locks its wheels and comes to a screeching halt.

Next stop, Greenwich Village.

****

She showed up at Leo's again a week later. Laurent was waiting for her. He had been waiting for a week. Could have waited a year, and it did feel like a year. She was wearing Gloria Vanderbilt jeans and a sleek, glove-leather bomber jacket – bright red, of course, but tastefully matte – from *The Cockpit*. He felt ashamed because the one he owned was made from very thick, almost unbendable cowhide, had a wooly collar and stretch material at the wrists and the waist, and came from a place near Pier 42 on Twelfth Avenue where you had to shake the metal shutters of a derelict store front repeatedly before they looked through a peephole and let you in. On the day

Fleur first spoke to him, he was glad he wore a tweed jacket, even if its elbows were threadbare.

Out of a sudden urge for privacy, they left Leo's where too many people might know them and had a quick meal of cheap steak and potatoes at *Tad's* in Times Square: although laughably kitsch, it was close by, she was in a rush and the plastic Tiffanesque lamps always made her laugh. "What a dump! A Liberace nightmare, almost as bad as the *Subway Inn*", she said mockingly, referring to that well-known heresy of drunken shabbiness in the spiffy Bloomingdale's neighborhood.

"You don't look like a regular of the *Subway Inn*"

She had a disarming smile, limpid and openly amused.

"A man proposed to me there".

"Did you accept?"

She didn't reply, made a dismissive gesture and a little pout.

"What is your name?", he asked.

"Call me Suzy".

"It is a hooker's name".

"I am shocked", she chuckled.

He paused, gathered his thoughts, wanted to say something deep and thoughtful to mark the occasion.

"I'm happy at last we can talk because I have been fascinated by something about you, something very unusual..."

She smiled again. How ordinary, trivial, pathetic! How many other men had been... fascinated?

Time to be more poetic.

"...something... floral, like a heady scent, juicy petals, and your clothes are the color of carnation like a flamenco dancer wears in her hair, with the same kind of vibrancy as the girl with the red hat in Kees Van Dongen's *The Corn Poppy*. So since flowers seem to be in order, may I call you "Fleur"? – which, quite fittingly, will also be a tribute to Sônia Braga in *Dona Flor and Her Two Husbands*, a movie I loved."

"That's a call girl's name", she said.

"That too".

Three metaphorical references in a row, no less, and insufferably pretentious. What a bore! He hated himself for how it all came out, but he meant every word he said, just couldn't express it candidly and genuinely enough. Maybe she would understand, wouldn't find those words so ridiculous after all, since they were coming out of a foreigner's mouth. And besides, girls are notoriously accepting and lenient, if they are nice and they like you.

She didn't mind her new name.

For a very short time, until their sinewy steaks and half-melted blobs of butter got to the table, she looked a bit uneasy, although still overwhelming Laurent with her presence and her charm. Only weeks later did he see a *Con Edison* invoice on her kitchen table and find out that her last name was Flores. Joyce Flores.

The name of a nice girl.

When they left *Tad's*, she hailed the first taxi on 42nd Street, gave Laurent a peck on the cheek and slipped a note in his hand. "Next Saturday, 7 PM, my place". On the back were her address and phone number.

****

Thirty-fourth Street, the next subway stop after 42nd, is one of Manhattan's lifelines. From East to West are the Empire State Building, then three department stores facing each other: Macy's, Gimbels and Korvettes, where hordes of Bridge-and-Tunnel people flock at Christmas time, trying to resurrect the spirit of "Miracle on 34th Street" and maybe catch a self-induced glimpse of Kris Kringle. West of that, closer to 8th Avenue, are Penn Station and the Madison Square Garden, then, on the right side of the avenue going South, is the landmark building of the United States Postal Service, a stately edifice with imposing colonnades that displays the most beautiful motto a postal service could ever boast: *"Neither snow nor rain nor heat nor gloom of night stays these couriers from the swift completion of their appointed rounds"*. Not that remarkable, his Moroccan friend Abidal told him once, since it was written five hundred years before Christ by Herodotus, in reference to the efficiency of the Persian messenger system. "The only person who should really be proud of this endorsement is the Shah of Iran", he said. Abidal is a philosopher, the closest thing to Diogenes the Cynic living in a barrel and occasionally holding a candle to search for an honest man – only his barrel is New York and his candle is a joint.

Thankfully, the Eighth-Avenue A train is an express that skips the 23rd Street station. One block East on 23rd is the Chelsea Hotel, where Bob Dylan kept a small suite for three years and Leonard Cohen had a one-night stand with Janis Joplin. Four small blocks South is Fleur's loft.

****

Laurent was relieved he didn't have to host: his tiny walk-up was outfitted with a king-size bed and he only had extra room for a table and one chair, so he ate in bed, worked in bed, watched TV in bed, did everything lying down. The first time he brought a woman to his place she tripped and flopped straight into bed as soon as she walked in, but that was the gig:

the practice of sex was harmless, playful and unconstrained, so this situation only brought a few laughs.

He would have felt horrible staging an encounter with Fleur in this fashion, not the least because of the shabbiness and ostentatiously lewd arrangement of his accommodation. In his mind, she was of quasi-divine essence, and an incapacity to greet her with all the required deference would have been blasphemous. He knew he often looked like an underpaid research associate, but actually that was not so bad. Showing himself to Fleur like an eternal student in a permanent frat party was inconceivable.

She welcomed him with a mischievous wink and a resounding "Hi, handsome!", then broke into a little girl's laugh at his astonishment. A harlot's words in a child's mouth, but still, a contagious laugh, and Laurent had to join in. She was more breathtaking than ever in a pair of Calvins and a rugby shirt, and had given up her trademark colors. "I'm taking a rest from myself", she said. He saw her glance at his lower section and retorted: "We guys only have Levis, Wranglers and Lees. Since I am not a gold-seeker or a cowboy, I can only wear Lees, the jeans of the factory worker. I have an industrial ass."

"I wasn't looking at your jeans", she said.

She lived in a beautifully renovated loft on 19th Street: 2,000 square feet, 14-foot columns, all in one big room with a huge semi-circular floor-to-ceiling window and, in one dark corner, a ridiculously small kitchen area: fridge on one side, stove on the other. When Laurent remarked about that singularity, she told him that of course she had asked the rental agent, but the only answer she got was a temperamental effeminate wriggle and a contemptuous dismissal: "Madam, when you can afford this kind of rent, you eat out."

"You still took it?"

"You bet."

They laughed again.

Her furniture was very basic but delightfully quirky: a glass coffee table with thick chrome legs, a red leather sofa in the shape of two huge lips, and a gigantic baseball glove for an armchair. "Straight from SoHo", she said. "I know someone who's going to open a store, maybe in a year or two. It'll be called *Think Big*. He gave me these samples, he thought that they would be free advertising in my place."

"He must like you a lot. And you must get a lot of traffic."

The walls were exquisitely decorated. In one section were Andy Warhol silkscreens of Mick Jagger and Marilyn Monroe and Roy Lichtenstein's giant comic strip panels, most notably his famous picture of a drowning girl, and in another the optical illusions of Yaacov Agam and Frank Stella. This is *so New York!* he thought, and wondered if they were originals. She seemed to have read his mind.

"Nice pieces, aren't they? I shouldn't blow my money on things like that."

He thought about his apartment where posters of "The Wiz" and "A Chorus Line" were pinned to the wall with thumbtacks and over the bed was an advertising sign he has stolen on the subway featuring women of all ages and all races with one sentence in Spanish: "El violador no distingue" (Rapists don't discriminate) and a telephone number to call. Quite a different planet. Occasionally, he ventured a timid critique, just to get a slight, temporary edge over someone he already knew he would soon be entirely subservient to. "There's not much of a view", he said. She shrugged her shoulders and replied: "The best view of the city is from Rykers island."

Rykers Island is the jail.

Maybe he could try talking about art.

"Op and Pop", he joked.

"Pardon me?"

"Yes. You managed to put together optical art and pop art... Very tasteful and very original."

She appreciated the compliment.

"I never thought of that... Speaking of pop, maybe you should open the bottle", she said.

He did and served his *Moët et Chandon* in little art deco Martini cups that were part of a Chase set. She said that the chrome kept the drinks colder. They toasted the evening.

"To Leo's and to us", he said.

She casually raised her cup.

"What are you doing hanging out at Leo's all the time?"

"I don't know. Nothing. Waiting for you, maybe."

"And what were you doing when you didn't know me?"

"Waiting for you. Even more. Without knowing."

She smiled again.

"Are you just a night owl or do you have a day job?"

"I am a journalist, which is what we in the business call an unemployed newspaper man. That said, I have a job. Or almost. And you?"

"Oh... I *know people*. I guess you could call it... PR..."

He paused, took a sip, let her put the flowers in a vase and some music on. Miles Davis. Did she know he had a love affair with Juliette Gréco in Paris? Maybe that's why she picked his music, maybe she was supremely knowledgeable, a lady of culture! Or there was still the possibility that she was just a flashy moron who had managed to seduce a wealthy businessman at San Juan's *Black Angus* and come to New York in his suitcase.

"Where do you come from?"

"Does it matter?"

"I'm sorry, I didn't mean to be inquisitive, it must be the journalist in me."

"When you've been here long enough, you will realize that coming to New York makes your whole past history irrelevant. Either you come *because* it was irrelevant in the first place but you didn't know, or it starts fading away as soon as you land here, and eventually gets totally erased. You reinvent yourself, you have to. You *get born* In New York, then you grow, feeding on the energy of the city, forever plugged into its buzz, until greatness becomes the new normal and you get bigger than life in your own eyes, you become your own myth. That's why everybody feels at home in New York: because home is here. For everybody. This is where we were all born, and this is where everything is… And there's no going back."

She was no moron.

"Is that why you came? To forget, to wipe the slate clean?"

"I don't remember. All I know is that here, you come from nowhere and you don't age."

"Is that why *I'm* here?… Is there a purpose to all this, you think?"

"Why don't you come and find out?"

She put her hands on his waist, pulled him gently towards her and kissed him.

"Now let's see if you deserve New York."

Five minutes later, he had forgotten his own name.

The next morning, he was born.

****

Laurent met Abidal in a taxi. In Morocco, Abidal was a philosophy professor. In New York, he eked out a living driving a Checker cab. They had a couple of drinks together, and when Laurent managed to get himself an interview with the new mayor of the city Ed Koch, he asked Abidal to help him finish a piece he was writing on CBGB, the new nightclub that served as the temple of punk rock, since Abidal lived close by in the East Village. When Laurent offered him the money he had promised for his work, Abidal refused to take it.

One night, Abidal rang his bell. Laurent put on his Lees and went downstairs to meet him. He just said: "Come."

They got in his Checker and he drove, a joint crackling under his thick moustache, not saying a word. The Fabulous Furry Freak Brothers. Laurent smiled at the thought. They went through the East Village and Avenues A, B, C and D, to the Lower East Side, to Orchard Street, Houston Street, the Bowery and Delancey, through Chinatown and Little Italy, and Abidal revealed treasures New York was reserving for its own kin, those people who were craving for intimacy with the city: magnificent murals with a wild poetic streak, little stores selling nothing and filled with crowds of noisy teenagers, and a night life beating to the rhythm of salsa and merengue. They passed in front of Abidal's place, jumping over the potholes at a dazzling speed, and Abidal said: "My place." He was squatting in a derelict building, hoping to take it over once the mandatory 10 years were up. Nobody seemed to know who the owner was, but one day developers might wake up and make a move, and on the other hand, well, they might not: after all, the whole southern part of Harlem along Central Park had been boarded up for years, and there was no sign of it ever becoming desirable enough for the new social class they would later call *Yuppie*.

Abidal stopped his taxi by the East River, facing Brooklyn, got off and leaned on the car, smoking and listening to the lapping of the waves. His eyes were glittering.

"You're not very talkative", Laurent observed.

"There's no need, just listen to New York talk", he said.

And a few seconds later, he added: "Her stories are a lot more interesting than ours."

In Abidal's mind, New York was a she.

When Abidal drove Laurent back, it was close to 4 AM.

Laurent never understood the meaning of that escapade.

****

West Fourth. Greenwich Village. Laurent heads South, passes by the basketball courts where the sweat of heroic feats makes the skin of black athletes shine beautifully in this summer evening, he stops for a few minutes to watch them jump to stellar height with the elegance and artistry of ballet dancers. Whether it is day or night has no meaning here, muscles can catch the faint flash of street lamps and glint any time. Further down is the Waverley Theater, where people are already lining up in costumes for the traditional midnight run of the Rocky Horror Picture Show. New York has taken ownership of this show, has made it hers. Rumor has it that one day, a shy, unassuming member of the audience started yelling at the characters of the movie for no particular reason, and then, in a spontaneous surge, people decided to dress as Eddie, Janet or Dr. Frank-N-Furter the transvestite, and to perform alongside the film, lip-syncing it, talking back to the actors and throwing projectiles at the screen. In true New York fashion, the show was not where it was supposed to be, but in the audience, on the street, in the act of collusion, in all of us, and for all of us to enjoy.

The Village that Fleur and Laurent had colonized between two flare-ups of sexual bulimia was not the Bleecker Street of the Figaro Café, at the corner of McDougall, where men and women of financial means were coming to buy a piece of bohemian life for an overpriced espresso, but further West, where you could savour a pizza at John's, then top it up with a *baba au rhum* with real rum at Rocco's Pasticceria diagonally across the street, listening to all brands and grades of Italian being hollered back and forth. And further still, there was the White Horse Tavern, resounding forever with the sound of the Clancy Brothers and haunted by the ghost of Jack *Ti-Jean* Kerouac, where Bob Dylan wooed Joan Baez and picked his stage name because it was the place where Dylan Thomas had had his last drunken binge before he went back to the Chelsea Hotel to die. Or there was the Pink Teacup, where you could gorge yourself on chitterlings, collard greens, black-eyed peas and corn fritters, while cockroaches on a mysterious migration would ragingly swing their antennae at you when they crossed the back of the booth where your lover had carelessly sat. The back of the booth on your side was probably worse, but at least you couldn't see it.

There were other oases with a special ambience, like Sullivan and Thompson Streets, outposts of Little Italy where mafia-operated "private clubs" abounded and Sicilian mamas dressed in black were knitting on folding chairs in the middle of the sidewalk, but Greenwich Village was also Gay City, and Christopher Street the Champs-Élysées of homosexuality, all the way to the Hudson River. Laurent and Fleur loved to barge in unexpectedly on the peaceful but cheerful life of that arts-oriented community, but maybe also get a cheap thrill casually walking by the Anvil, a gay BDSM sex club with fierce-looking characters in leather and chains always on the look-out.

"They seem to like your industrial ass", she told him.

****

127

Once Laurent got over the initial ravishment of their first love fest, he found himself increasingly powerless and overwhelmed. In Fleur's book he may have just been born, and maybe that is why she made him feel constantly needy, cold and hungry. In front of her he always seemed hopelessly naked and fragile – and starving, whether for her affection or driven by the avid desire just to fuse himself to her womb, terrified that he might experience pain post-partum. Why such a breathtaking beauty whose explosive youth was consumed by the wealthiest gentlemen and probably coveted by the handsomest would take an interest in him and put up with his natural gaucheness and his threadbare tweed jacket was something he simply could not comprehend. She surely had a hidden agenda, ulterior motives, maybe she would slap him with a bill, who knows… When he decided to open up, playing coy at first, but then complaining to her semi-facetiously about being just an ugly duckling "oppressed by the figures of beauty", she instantly recognized the song, had a little laugh and completed his statement by paraphrasing its lyrics, written by another illustrious guest of the Chelsea Hotel: "I prefer handsome men, but for you I will make an exception."

Like Abidal, Fleur, although not an introvert by any means, was by nature the quiet sort. When Laurent asked her during one of his regular insecurity attacks why she was so reluctant to open up and show her feelings, she replied: "There's no need, because I'm just one of the iterations of the marvelous things you see all around. It's when couples stop climaxing that they start talking", and with an engaging expression, she added: "and this is New York, so I am climaxing all the time."

Whenever Fleur bothered to use language for communication, she related to it the same way as she related to everything else: with profound originality, playfulness and grace, inventing words at her leisure or twisting their meaning to create a vernacular of her own. It took a while for Laurent to understand that whenever she talked about "fun", she meant "sex", and whenever she said: "You're so silly", she meant: "This is hilarious." And effectively, she would focus on silliness and fun, while serving as a sounding board to the constant humming of the city, its generosity and its demands. At times she was also a lightning rod, igniting magic and insanity through simple poetic words, her smooth body seemingly swimming though life like a mermaid's. New York was grateful for this and reciprocated with fiery synergy: she was the most radiant spokesperson the city could have, and in turn the beauty and power of the city echoed and amplified her own.

There is an intelligence of the body, the way it has of alighting, unfolding, instinctively picking, out of millions of different configurations or inclinations, the one that will produce the greatest aesthetic or sensual joy. Fleur's body was graced with that kind of intelligence to the highest degree. How surprisingly unperceptive of women to ignore it, Laurent often thought, looking at Fleur reading a magazine or rearranging her hair with pins in her mouth, when it is so rare, so precious, so... spiritual, and the other kind of intelligence, the one that dwells in the encephalon and its cream cheese texture for which they so crave to be loved, is so mundane, widespread, overrated. The syntax of desire feeds on the intelligence of the body. Desire has its own grammar, its declensions, its conjugations using such auxiliaries as the insignificant curvature of an instep or the fugitive abandonment of an unconcerned neckline. It creates a language filtered through the senses which reaches its full potential in that sublime contact by which the male reveals his brutal but paltry and futile compulsion to penetrate and get to the bottom of everything, whereas the female, who holds the secret of life without understanding it, feels unfathomable and rejoices in her own mystery. So desire would get a hold of Laurent and take him away, wave by wave, always further, always stronger. And even when he emerged, suffocating, crazed with love and intensity, he would marvel at the weary heaviness of her legs, which glistened with the nobility of a high-strung mare after a race.

This is what he learned from Fleur. And she did not even have to explain.

****

By now, Laurent has reached SoHo, another part of the city to which he wants to bid farewell before he commits the irreparable. He didn't realize that it was getting very late and now the streets are empty, his only companion is the echo of his Frye boots on the cobblestones of Broome and Green Streets.

He loves SoHo because it is what New York is all about: a spontaneously generated surge, an uncontrollable tidal wave which presented humanity with a *fait accompli* and set a new standard for generations to come. SoHo is as close as one can get to true anarchic greatness.

In the middle of the 19th century, just before the steel era, multi-storey warehouses and huge workshops were built in this part of the city, and the material used for cladding was cast iron, which was strong and malleable and lent itself to sumptuous motifs, friezes and decorative columns in the French and Italian classical styles. A century or so later, because taxation got too high and the city too densely populated to ensure the timely transportation of the goods manufactured on site, the district was gradually abandoned and companies moved to New Jersey or other adjoining areas.

As natures abhors a void, just a few years before Laurent's arrival, the artistic community became attracted to those deserted building, which offered at little cost very desirable, unique features: huge spaces, oversized windows, lofty ceilings, hardwood floors, and they started squatting in them. Who cared that there were no stores and the zoning was commercial? Who cared it was all illegal? Those people were drifters, bohemians, beggars, and beggars can't be choosers.

They first used those places as studios, but then they refurbished them, put their paintings and sculptures in them and made them their own private galleries, spit-shined the wood floors inch by inch and repainted the acanthus leaves of the Corinthian columns a dark green, built bedrooms, added bathrooms and kitchens, put in Dolby stereo, had babies. And before the cumbersome bureaucracy of a metropolis the population of Canada could get their act together and evict them, too many bohemians had moved in.

So all of a sudden, after years of threatening and indecisive bitching, the bureaucracy became pragmatic, the city let the bohemians stay and simply changed the zoning. And then, a bit later, the whole neighbourhood was awarded the status of National Historical Landmark. The street, the people had won again, aestheticism, creativity and inventiveness prevailed, lunacy became supreme wisdom, bohemians woke up one day owning multi-million-dollar estates and New York had launched the world-wide loft movement.

It is starting to drizzle, and Laurent's boots are echoing louder on the cobblestones of the cast iron gorges. There used to be music on Clinton Street all through the evening. What happened to it?

He will skip Tribeca, Wall Street and the World Trade Center in his pilgrimage: ant hills in the daytime, dead mausoleums at night.

He veers East, where he knows there will be people again.

****

The minute she opened her arms to him, the whole city gushed in.

Fleur was a compulsive "entertainee", and all she apparently wanted out of life was to be amused. To her credit, everything amused her, and she had happily opted to live in a place where entertainment was everywhere: in theatres, in concert halls, in subway stations, in the parks, in the streets..., so she was in perfect harmony with the environment she had chosen. A refreshing thought, for Laurent, was that this constant thirst for pleasure was not the obsession of a superficial mind, but the quest of a real hedonist, who had made it her life's purpose and philosophy. But conversely, Laurent always questioned why she had chosen him to share a slice of life with, and he could not settle for the simple explanation that in the best case scenario he might be just a pastime, and in the worst he served as the queen's jester. He was claiming to be a lover, dark and tormented, and rejected the perfunctory role he felt he was playing, so he began to suspect that if he certainly was a desperate, hopeless romantic, he was no hedonist, but at best just an aspiring epicurean. He knew that being a hedonist would have been easier, and that scared him, so dark and tormented he was.

One day, he thought he was being clever by answering one of her blunt invitations to "have sex" with the words: "*I don't 'have sex', I make love*". She paused for a second and said good-humouredly: "Okay. Let's just fuck, then." This was an aplomb· he did not have.

And meanwhile, insidiously, the city was penetrating him and settling in his own psyche: through every exposure to the street and the crowds, but also every Broadway show, every movie, every piece of architectural wonder, and the millions of things that he was doing with Fleur, which inevitably triggered passionate reactions in both of them. However unstable and ill-defined their love was, it went through a state of grace: she demanded entertainment and companionship and he provided them, while the city demanded to take possession of Laurent, and she was teaching him how to be possessed.

Fleur had an instant intuition of how to show the right composure in any kind of situation; she blended with everything she chose to blend with, while her incredible beauty would still stand out but impose itself as an indispensable feature of her staying on the scene, and she treated Laurent with great tenderness and amusement when he showed an inability to act the part. One evening, when they were lining up at the door of Studio 54 in the hope of going in to catch a glimpse of Mick Jagger or Andy Warhol like thousands of other people did, the notoriously disturbed doorman Marc Benecke invited her to go in but would not admit him – so they left, and Fleur tried to say a few comforting words to boost his wounded ego.

"Don't worry about it, he's crazy, you know, and permanently stuffed with cocaine… They say he even turned away Cher and Frank Sinatra. He's one of the attractions of Studio 54, a little like Edsel Fong, that abusive San Francisco waiter who greets his customers with a "Sit down and shut up", then curses them, spills soup in their laps and makes overt sexual advances to them. It's all part of the ritual of obnoxiousness, which is almost an art form in New York."

"But what is it that he did not like about me?"

"Who knows? It probably was purely subjective, or maybe he sensed you didn't have the right attitude…"

"And what's that?"

"Just… *attitude*, you know… You have to look… very *New York*…"

"And what's *that*?"

"An elaborate mix of sarcasm, a "know-it-all" style, intellectual and aesthetic sophistication, with a tad of eccentricity and a sense of entitlement, like you own the place – you have to be self-confident, show some *chutzpah*, without being (too) arrogant or confrontational… and have a sense of humor. It's all in the dosage: a drop of this, two pinches of that, shake it well, and make it all come out through your eyes, in the way you look at people…"

"Was that what you were doing?"

"No. I don't have to."

"Why?"

"I'm the right kind of beauty."

"Which is…?"

"Spectacular."

That night, Laurent dreamed that the herringbone weave of his tweed jacket was being burnt into his flesh with a branding iron.

But New York seemed to always know how to redeem itself: a week later, his poor man's bomber jacket did not raise a single eyebrow when they went to CBGB to see Talking Heads and Blondie. She told him that he should go take a look at the men's room, that it was to CBGB what Andy Warhol was to Studio 54.

Laurent stayed in the men's room at CBGB, his mouth agape, for at least 20 minutes, just looking around. Every inch of the place, walls and ceiling, was covered with hundreds of intricate networks of multicoloured graffiti, and only the white urinals and toilets were spared, standing alone like obscene utilitarian exhibits in a gallery where art was everywhere else, as though Jackson Pollock had been hired as its interior decorator. In New York, Pop Art – the real one, the art of the street and the people – had no qualms about being down and dirty.

When Laurent sat in his seat, he looked at Fleur and she looked back at him.

Her eyes expressed nothing but pure beauty and collusion. He loved her for that.

****

Just in time!

One of their rituals would be to go have razor clams and lobsters in black bean sauce in Chinatown, then cross Canal Street and finish the evening with a cappuccino and a pastry at Ferraro's in Little Italy. The Sun Hop Kee is getting ready to close, Laurent may have ten minutes left but he's not hungry. He still walks down Mott instinctively, to experience the industriousness of the street and be blinded by the over-lit windows of Chinese restaurants one last time. His melancholy has left him. He knows that there will be more Chinatowns and that they will all be the same. The drizzle has stopped. He feels at peace.

When he gets to Chatham Square, he realizes that this is the end of the line, that he is no longer on Fleur's turf. The Lower East Side can be creepy, even sleazy at times. The Bowery is entirely populated by panhandlers, which has always surprised Laurent because in his mind it defeats the very purpose of panhandling, but go figure... One day he was walking in the street for God knows what reason and asked the only person in decent attire if he had the time. The man gave him all his change and ran away.

"It must be your accent", Fleur told him.

And then there is that vast amorphous Jewish world extending all along Orchard Street, past Delancey and back to Houston Street, ending at Katz's delicatessen. After that is Abidal's East Village, very poor and very Puerto Rican, where it isn't even safe to walk in the daytime, let alone at night.

Fleur has always hated shabbiness: she only ventured to Laurent's apartment a couple of times, and only because it was close to Leo's, and slept over once, after they had gotten stoned out of their minds in a huge Times Square movie theatre draped in red vervet, watching Andy Warhol's "Dracula" in 3-D. She was deeply depressed by the open-air displays of thrift and junk along Orchard Street and the gloom of the surrounding area. Hester Street, Delancey are not a part of her world, which only extends South of Houston through occasional forays into SoHo, Little Italy and Chinatown. The rest of the area is made up of a constellation of oases: Katz's, CBGB…, connected by taxis.

The sadness is getting to him again. He peers into the back streets, raises his hand while still walking, looks for a cab. There is one in the distance. He hopes that it is a Checker.

It is a Checker.

****

Alcohol and cannabis soon became a part of the scene. They appeared out of nowhere and felt like they had always been there. A couple of evenings a week, Fleur would dress to the nines and disappear, and Laurent knew better than to ask where. On those days, he avoided Leo's but could not work, so he sometimes stayed in his apartment but mostly at Fleur's, smoking a joint, watching sitcoms on cable TV and slugging cognac out of a bottle to amplify the ponderous waves of foggy numbness which the cannabis slowly pushed through his muscles and into his mind.

Sometimes he cried.

When she came back, she would kick her shoes off and join him, and they would laugh too loud at Vinnie Barbarino or Archie Bunker. They never made love on those evenings. They never fucked either.

What was the primary nature of his intoxication, the nucleus around which the others gravitated? Alcohol? Marijuana? New York? – or was it the most beautiful woman in the world, which at least was a bearable thought? All he knew was that he had just been forced out of a protracted, comfortably sane infancy in a faraway land, and straight into what might well have been his youth, but which was even more confusing and already burning itself out from its own intensity. Maybe Laurent was just lifting his glass to the awful truth which you can't reveal to the ears of youth, except to say it isn't worth a dime. But that song had not been written yet.

Soon would come closure time. It had to.

****

The Checker cab is a New York institution, another icon of the city, a standard feature of every movie, every TV series, and Robert de Niro has given it mythical status in Martin Scorsese's masterpiece. It has been around since the Roaring Twenties, subtly changing its looks as different historical periods imposed new aesthetic lines and volumes. The current design dates back to the late 1950s and has not changed since then. The car has a massive 8-cylinder engine and can accommodate eight occupants: three in the front, three in the back and two on folding stools facing the back seat. Its strictly utilitarian greyish dashboard looks like the command post of a U-Boat. The Checker Motors Corporation, based in Kalamazoo, Michigan, is in fact just another assembly line in a satellite of Detroit: its cabs use a Chevy engine and every other part is sub-contracted to independent manufacturers. Its genius has been to promote a brand and an image, with little substance. The energy crisis and the obsession to keep cab fares low have made such a large, heavy vehicle much less profitable, and new limits imposed by the city to the number of passengers a taxi can hold have dealt Checker another blow. The Checker cab is a dinosaur, just waiting for the slightest quake to receive the *coup de grâce*.

Laurent stretches his legs and he cannot even touch the back of the driver's cabin. What a luxury! Recently, he has switched to Bourbon, he thinks it smells like the New York subway. He takes the flask out of his pocket. The cab driver looks at him in his rear-view mirror but says nothing. His name is Michel Jean, he is Haitian, probably left his country when *Bébé Doc* came to power and when his protégé Lucker Cambronne, the head of the *Tontons Macoutes* nicknamed "the Vampire of the Caribbean", was extorting five tons of blood plasma a month from peasants to sell it to US labs. On the dashboard is a picture of soccer star Arsène Auguste, another *émigré* who showed brilliance playing for Tampa Bay against the New York Cosmos and living legend Pelé. Maybe Laurent should start a conversation. A month ago, he would have written a story about it, sent it to *Le Journal*. He was more inspired than ever, everything in New York deserved covering, every individual story was an epic, or if it wasn't, it deserved to be one.

Was New York the brew from which all life emerged and where all life ended? At some point, Laurent was close to believing it, even though his life in New York was coming to an end.

He lights a joint. The driver too.

"313 West 48th Street, *s'il vous plaît*"

"*Oui, Monsieur.*"

The cab responds with a tired, mangey old lion's roar, and pulls out with a sudden, unexpectedly strong thrust, all metals grinding and shaking.

He remembers another taxi ride a few weeks earlier.

"Let's go have a picnic at the Cloisters", Fleur had said.

"Where?"

"The Cloisters. You'll see, you'll like it".

The cab driver was a jovial 50-year-old predictably named Seamus O'Something who made no secret about having fled Northern Ireland because of his tempestuous political activism and all the skeletons his overflowing closets were coughing up at an ever-growing pace on British authorities. His legend would have largely overshadowed, both by its humour and its tragic insanity, such flamboyant fictional heroes as Travis Bickle, or even Louie De Palma and the characters played by Andy Kaufman or Christopher Lloyd in the TV series. As usual, in New York, reality surpassed fiction.

"The Cloisters? *Oy* live close *boy*. A wonderful neighbourhood indeed", and he added: "and Cathluck too!".

The cab went up Madison Avenue through the Upper East Side, its art galleries, spiffy advertising agencies and luxurious charities, and then, as it made its way North, the neighbourhood became less opulent and the buildings insidiously more modest, then shabby, then run down. By the time it made a left turn on Central Park North/110th Street, the taxi had driven a few blocks into East Harlem already. The windows of all the buildings facing Central Park were blocked by sheets of plywood as developers were waiting for the right time, the right amount of expropriations, the right dose of gentrification to start making money. Meanwhile, they bought up everything that was worth a dime. Bought up, boarded up and waited up, because the city never sleeps. They waited up for decades while their properties were plunged in deep slumber.

Further along 110th Street is an enclave in Spanish Harlem: St. John the Divine, the largest Anglican cathedral in the world. Seamus summarily mimicked the sign of the cross, kissed his thumb and cursed at the same time.

St. John the Divine's construction started in *La Belle Époque*. Three quarters of a century later it is not finished and it will never be. The extravagance and hubris of the concept demand that all reliefs, gargoyles, sculptures and architectural details be hand-crafted by the finest artisans and those experts are a dying breed, so every year the managers of the project have to go deeper into Italy or France to find the proper talents, at a higher cost each time. They put them up, give them room and board and a luxurious stipend, and when the endowment runs out, the project is suspended until more money can be found. Right now it is suspended.

West Harlem. Five miles of thick Hispanic life, complete with food, music and street bustle. Although *West Side Story*, the New York *Romeo and Juliet*, was staged a little bit further south, this is where Laurent pictured it. In New York, poverty means danger, and West Harlem is dangerous. On 155th Street and Broadway is one of those incongruous places with which New York likes to surprise us: the Museum of the American Indian, the most extraordinary collection of Santa Clara pottery, Hopi kachina dolls, Sioux costumes, Navajo rugs, Pueblo sand paintings and thousands of precious artifacts of incalculable cultural, artistic and historical value. The museum, bookstore and gift shop are always empty. Only a few yellow school buses can be seen at times in the parking lot, most often with New Jersey plates.

Then is Sugar Hill: magnificent brownstones and massive Gothic apartment buildings where rich black people live: a surprising area of affluence amidst a vast display of urban indigence, and a gravitational field for successful heroes of the jazz culture.

When they arrived in Washington Heights, Seamus proudly announced: "*Moy* Neighbourhood" and stopped the cab, politely but authoritatively asking them to get off.

"Why? We're not at the Cloisters yet", said Fleur.

"Because it is worth a stop."

And indeed it was.

Besieged by an ever-advancing Dominican community, there was a small Irish village nestled around a few astonishing buildings with an art deco cachet of the highest quality: lobbies of shiny white metal and marble, insanely high ceilings, stained glass with elongated geometrical motifs, huge mirrors and decorative columns, wall sconces and vertical chandeliers of molded glass, it was like stepping into the world of Fred Astaire and Ginger Rogers.

Fleur simply noted: "Even *I* did not know about this wonder!"

Past the George Washington bridge, on top of a hill and surrounded by a park, was the end of their ride: the Met Cloisters.

Even in France Laurent had heard about it, but he was far from imagining what he would see.

Owned by the Metropolitan Museum of Art, it featured a museum of medieval art housed in five religious structures built in the Middle Ages that were dismantled stone by stone in the South West of France and reassembled at the northern tip of Manhattan, with a sweeping view of the Hudson river. That feat was the dream of Paris-trained sculptor and art dealer George Grey Barnard, who managed to pull it off almost single-handedly, on his own dime, and then came additional funding and donations by John D. Rockefeller and J.P. Morgan who bought into the dream.

George Grey Barnard died a couple of weeks before the Cloisters' official opening.

After a brief visit of the museum, Laurent and Fleur found an ideal place for their tablecloth on the grounds of the complex and had a deferential, demure picnic of *pâté de campagne*, fresh fruit and Châteauneuf-du-Pape from Sherry-Lehmann, hidden in a brown paper bag as required under penalty of law in one of the world capitals of crime, sex and drugs. They leisurely chattered while a slight breeze from the Hudson played with Fleur's hair, which she had ravishingly let fall on her shoulders and frame her face. She was more beautiful than she had ever been, and Laurent thought no-one could ever be more. That exquisite, blissful fleeting moment was a minute of eternity which kept forever a very special place in Laurent's memory.

"This definitely needs a bit of... irreverence."

She had broken the spell – but had she? The spell had to be broken anyway, and lust, although a dead end, was the least arduous, most conventional way out – a delusional escape, but an escape all the same, and pleasure was an early retribution of future pain.

"How?"

"Well, let's have fun!"

And fun they had, first under a tree, then on the grass in the middle of an open area, immersed in their pleasure and oblivious of their surroundings. They were not disturbed or interrupted and did not have to wrap themselves in a brown paper bag.

On that day, Laurent felt wholeheartedly free and happy, in total harmony with Fleur's every move, anticipating her most intimate reflexes and carried away by the magnificence of the premises and the magnitude of his own desire. And in return, the intelligence of Fleur's body at rest turned into sheer brilliance in motion, and as usual, the stupidity of his desire was justified by the refinement of its cause. Little did he know that it would be his last moment of absolute fulfillment, of unrestricted wonderment, their swan song.

His descent into hell, or at least its kitchen, did not take long. On the way back downtown, they could not get a Checker cab and had to settle for a Dodge Coronet, a kind of long, flat cigar with no leg room reeking of cigarette butts and vulgarity. They went down Broadway silently and interminably, then on to Central Park West, past the *Dakota* where John Lennon lived and *Rosemary's baby* had been shot, past *Tavern on the Green*, which Warner LeRoy had just renovated and illegally expanded at a cost of 10 million dollars, and past the *Majestic*, home to Lucky Luciano, Meyer Lansky and the Genovese crime family. Fleur insisted on taking an indirect, alternate route to her place, along Central Park South to see the carriages waiting for tourists and their horses defecating out of sheer boredom directly across from the magnificent, turn-of-the-century French renaissance-style Plaza Hotel. On the left they briefly spotted *À la Vieille Russie*, a store relocated from Paris and loaded with Fabergé art pieces and antique Russian imperial treasures, then veered South on Fifth Avenue.

Fleur did not feel like spending the night with Laurent, so she dropped him off at Rockefeller Center, across the street from St. Patrick's cathedral.

Absurdly, Laurent thought that somehow he might bump into Seamus.

Such are Laurent's thoughts as a cab driver named Michel Jean takes him back to Hell's Kitchen.

****

When did the ground start to shift under his feet? Was it at the same time as the panic attacks started? It must have been right after the Blackout. While the city was in the grips of the Son of Sam and everybody was wondering how many people their next-door neighbour had killed, all lights went out for 48 hours, sirens started blaring, store windows got smashed and shadows were running around with stereo sets and boomboxes under their arms. Laurent had taken refuge at Fleur's place because he could not stand the heat of Hell's Kitchen, which had been turned up a few notches to make the devil feel more at home. Still, on those two evenings at Fleur's, while people were howling in the street like wolves or cackling out their witches' curses, Fleur's improvised candle-lit affairs felt more like black masses on the island of Dr. Moreau than intimate dinners at the Great Gatsby's. The New York blackout took place on July 13 and 14. July 14 is Bastille Day. *Vive la France!*

Yes, that must have been when the feeling of fear and entrapment started. On one side, Laurent felt that he was being absorbed, digested by the madness of New York, and on the other side Fleur's beauty was obliterating him by its unarguable absoluteness, so the very pleasure she was giving him he increasingly perceived as an instrument of domination, all the more powerful because he could not resist it. In this crossfire, Fleur and New York were two extensions of the same huge organic mass vested with a mysterious mission and conspiring to melt him into a new, unknown entity, or at least one that at such an early stage of his morphing he did not recognize. When did sex and vampirism merge? When did energy turn into dark matter? Of course, his unrestricted use of Bourbon and cannabis, initially to take "the edge" off, whatever it was, became instrumental in designing this new hell, and even after the mysterious Son of Sam David Berkowitz got caught, the city kept running a high fever and so did he. New York was definitely out of control, but New York was always on the cusp of madness, it was just a matter of knowing which kind of madness was prevalent at one juncture or another. At least New York's madness was in the image of the city: powerful and shameless, whereas Laurent's was sheepish, born of a deep chasm between his desperate will to comply and conform and his equally desperate determination to stay whole.

When insane serial killer David Berkowitz got caught, he greeted the police with words that only a New Yorker could have pronounced:

"What took you so long?"

****

Laurent does not want to go home right away, not yet, so he asks Michel Jean to drop him off at the *Metropole*. It is the longest bar in the city, probably about thirty or forty feet, and exotic dancers in platform shoes lazily try to shimmy and writhe on the copper top. The place got bombed for no apparent reason a few years ago, which adds to its lure and its mystery. He sits in front of the most attractive girl, stuffs a few bucks in her undies and orders a double Wild Turkey on the rocks.

DANIEL SOHA

Through his descent into his personal hell, Fleur appeared perfectly normal, he recalls. Was he so totally mistaken, so thoroughly paranoid? But didn't the witches' coven in *Rosemary's Baby* appear normal too? Of course, he thought he got a glimpse of her secret garden when her eyes looked redder and wetter than usual as she was listening to Judy Collins' version of *Both Sides Now*, but could he trust his own eyes, which by that time had turned redder and wetter than hers?

When she announced that she was getting married, his immediate reaction, for a split second, was to think quite absurdly that it would be with him. But no: she mentioned some wealthy financier in Connecticut...

"So you lied to me..."

"Did I?"

"You said there was no going back."

"I'm not going back. I'm going... *elsewhere*."

"But why?"

"For many reasons. Our relationship consumed itself, like New York consumed us..."

"New York? I thought New York and you had a pact, that I was just a distraction. New York... consumed us?..."

"And it was delightful, but this is the end of the line. It is New York, and when New York has consumed you, there is no appeal."

"No going back..."

"Exactly."

"What should I do? I love you, you know, consumed or not..."

"Keep the memory, darling, and make it work for you, make it enrich your life. Life has decided that we should leave each other when we are both still in love, so we will not go through the torture of quibbling endlessly in a state of lovelessness, nor

146

weigh the assets and liabilities of an emotional balance sheet that's already moot. I have chosen my own agonies and my own raptures. Try to find yours."

He should have gone after her, maybe pleaded, maybe debased himself. He didn't. He just mentioned, conventionally and boringly, that they should have... talked about it.

"We never did too much talking anyway", she said.

****

What was this story all about? Boy meets girls, boy loves girl and girl loves boy, then life has another agenda in store for them. What would have happened if their love had unfolded among haystacks, between slag heaps – or worse: between *Le Chemin des Dames* and *Verdun*, between *Le Chambon-sur-Lignon*, Switzerland and Vichy? What was the part New York played in its flamboyance, in its magnificence? How did New York beautify it, glorify it, and was it even glorious?

Was it even love?

Laurent leaves the *Metropole* and walks back to his apartment. The suitcases are ready, in the middle of the floor. He is leaving tomorrow. He has left a message on Abidal's answering machine, so maybe the Moroccan will take him to the airport. Is it wise to prolong the agony? Probably not, but he has to keep simmering in it, at least for a while, out of respect for Fleur and her panache. He knows he will not sleep tonight. Maybe they will play "Superman" on the flight back.

****

Later, he will take control of his own narrative, and never let a city tell his story again – maybe he will have gotten stronger

147

and maybe not, but all other places will be weak, slumped along some functional or befouled waterway, following the same playbook again and again, or just sprawling haphazardly and endlessly. New York was the only city standing, the only city that could be the hero of a story, Céline knew that already in 1932.

Laurent will spend a lifetime in exile, a deserter and a renegade, away from his home but never recognizing it as such when he was there, and the city will keep living without him, reinventing itself and never ageing, unrecognizable but inexorably recreating Fleur for other men. He will go through marriage, career, children, and write many other stories searching for the beauty and the greatness he had already found but casually let go because he thought they were now part of him and they would automatically follow.

But no, beauty is not in the eyes of the beholder. Beauty is a choice and a value.

Like courage.

Years later, he will still wonder whether it was the youth of humanity that went down the drain in Hell's Kitchen on that ominous night, or just his own.

And if it was just his own, why did it only last eighteen months?

APPENDIX

FROM "THE PRODUCERS" TO "TAXI": A DOZEN YEARS THAT MADE NEW YORK

1967: EVENTS

Riots in Harlem, the South Bronx and Brooklyn following the killing of a Puerto Rican man by the police
Death of Edward Hopper in his Washington Square studio.
Andy Warhol's Marilyn Monroe series
Release of "The Fixer", by Bernard Malamud. Pulitzer Prize and national Book Award

MOVIES:

"The Producers" (Director: Mel Brooks – With Gene wilder and Zero Mostel)
"The Odd Couple" (Director: Gene Saks – With Walter Matthau and Jack Lemon). Premiere at Radio City Music Hall

MUSIC/DANCE

Concert by Barbra Streisand in Central Park

1968: EVENTS

Riots in Harlem and Brooklyn after the assassination of Martin Luther King
First appearance of community murals in East Harlem, the South Bronx and the Lower East Side
Assassination attempt on Andy Warhol at his studio *The Factory* by radical feminist Valerie Solanas

MOVIES
"Flesh" (Producer: Andy Warhol – Director: Paul Morissey – With Joe Dalessandro)

"Funny Girl" (Director: William Wyler – With Barbra Streisand and Omar Sharif)

"Rosemary's Baby" (Director: Roman Polanski – With Mia Farrow and John Cassavetes), in the Dakota building

MUSIC/DANCE
Leonard Cohen and Janis Joplin have a one-night stand at the Chelsea Hotel

TELEVISION/TV RELEASES
Start of "The Dick Cavett Show": 2,000 hours of programming, more than 5,000 interviews, until 1980

THEATRE/MUSICALS
"The Indian Wants the Bronx" (With Al Pacino, John Cazale and Marsha Mason)(Off Broadway)

1969: EVENTS
Gay riots at the Stonewall Inn
Release of "Portnoy's Complaint", by Philip Roth

MOVIES
"Midnight Cowboy" (Director: John Schlesinger, with Dustin Hoffman and John Voight)

"Hello Dolly" (Director: Gene Kelly – With Barbra Streisand, Louis Armstrong, Walter Matthau)

"Goodbye, Columbus" (Director: Larry Peerce – With Richard Benjamin and Ali McGraw – From Philip Roth)

World release at the Fine Arts Theatre of "They Shoot Horses, Don't They?" (S. Pollack, Jane Fonda, M. Sarrazin)

MUSIC:
Release of "I Guess the Lord Must Be in New York City", by Harry Nilsson, initially intended for "Midnight Cowboy"

SPORTS:
New York Jets win the Superbowl with quarterback Joe Namath

1970: <u>EVENTS</u>

Christopher Street Liberation Day (first anniversary of Stonewall riots and first Gay Parade)

Retrospective of Frank Stella's work at the Museum of Modern Art (he was 34 years old at the time)

· <u>MOVIES</u>

"Trash" (Producer: Andy Warhol – Director: Paul Morissey – With Joe Dalessandro)

"The Landlord" (Director: Hal Ashby – With Jeff Bridges)

"High, Mom!" (Director: Brian de Palma – With Robert De Niro)

<u>MUSIC/DANCE</u>

Birth of street dancing in the Bronx (first hip-hop, then breakdance)

Release of "Sweet Jane" (The Velvet Underground, Lou Reed)

Opening of Jimi Hendrix's "Electric Lady Studios" (5th Avenue and 8th Street).

Jimi Hendrix records his last piece: "Slow Blues", at Electric Lady Studios

<u>SPORTS</u>

New York Knicks win the NBA championship

<u>TELEVISION/TV RELEASES</u>

"The Odd Couple", with Tony Randall and Jack Klugman (until 1975)

1971: <u>EVENTS</u>

Donald Trump becomes president of Trump Management

Center of graffiti culture shifts from Philadelphia to Washington Heights/the Bronx, then to the whole subway system

Amendment of the Zoning Resolution allowing artists to live in SoHo lofts

Alexander Calder unveils his Bent Propeller sculpture at the World Trade Center

Opening of the Exxon Building

<u>MOVIES</u>

"Carnal Knowledge" (Director: Mike Nichols – With Jack Nicholson, Art Garfunkle)

"The French Connection" (Director: William Friedkin – With
   Gene Hackman and Roy Scheider)

MUSIC/DANCE
Closing of the Gas Light Café in Greenwich Village. (Bob Dylan
   and Bruce Springsteen were regulars)
Release of "Sonida Bestial" by Puerto Rican "Kings of Salsa" Ricardo
   Ray and Bobby Cruz (Vaya Records)
John Lennon moves to New York

TELEVISION/TV RELEASES
"All in the Family", with Carroll O'Connor, Jean Stapleton and Rob
   Reiner (until 1979)

1972: EVENTS
Opening of "The Duchess", first lesbian bar in New York, across the
   street from the Stonewall Inn

MOVIES
"The Godfather" (Director: Francis Ford Coppola – With Marlon
   Brando, Al Pacino, James Caan)
"Klute" (Director: Alan Pakula – With Jane Fonda and Donald
   Sutherland)
"Heat" (Producer: Andy Warhol – Director: Paul Morissey – With
   Joe Dalessandro)
"Deep Throat" (Director: Gerard Damiano – With Linda Lovelace)

MUSIC/DANCE
Opening of "La Fille du Régiment" at the Metropolitan Opera.
   Luciano Pavarotti becomes a star
Release of "Walk on the Wild Side" (Lou Reed)

THEATRE/MUSICALS
"The Sunshine Boys"
"The River Niger"
"6 Rms Riv Vu"

1973: EVENTS

Bomb explodes at the "Metropole" topless bar (7th Avenue and 48th Street). No casualties

The Trump Organization is sued for violating the 1968 Fair Housing Act (refusing to rent to black people)

Marcel Duchamp retrospective at the Museum of Modern Art

Opening of the twin towers of the World Trade Center, highest buildings in the world (415 and 417 meters)

Andy Warhol's *Mao* series

Designation of SoHo as a landmark and creation of the SoHo-Cast Iron Historic District

Opening of the McGraw-Hill Building

MOVIES:

"The Way We Were" (Director – Sydney Pollack – With Barbra Streisand and Robert Redford)

"The Devil in Miss Jones" (Director: Gerard Damiano – With Georgina Spelvin)

"Flesh for Frankenstein" (Producer: Andy Warhol – Director: Paul Morissey – With Joe Dalessandro)

"Mean Streets". (Director: Martin Scorsese – With Harvey Keitel)

"Serpico" (Director: Sidney Lumet – With Al Pacino)

MUSIC/DANCE

DJ Kool Herc, a Jamaican immigrant, invents rap music in the Bronx, by scratching James Brown records

John Lennon moves into the Dakota building, on Central Park West, where *Rosemary's Baby* was shot

Opening of music club "CBGB" on the Bowery

Release of "Piano Man", by Billy Joel

THEATRE/MUSICALS

"The Rocky Horror Show"

SPORTS:

New York Knicks win the NBA championship

1974: EVENTS

Election of Democrat Abraham Beame in replacement of John Lindsay. First Jewish mayor of New York City

Opening of gay/BDSM/sex club The Anvil (14th Street and 10th Avenue)

Acquittal of New York mobster Meyer Lansky ("The Mafia's Accountant") of tax evasion in Miami

First high-profile case won by Rudy Giuliani (Southern District of New York) for bribery of Assemblyman Bert Podell

Opening of restaurant "Le Cirque"

MOVIES:

"Death Wish" (Director: Michael Winner – With Charles Bronson)

The Godfather Part II" (Director: Francis Ford Coppola – With Al Pacino, Robert de Niro, Robert Duvall)

"Blood for Dracula" (Producer: Andy Warhol – Director: Paul Morissey – With Joe Dalessandro)

"Claudine" (Director: John Berry – With James Earl Jones and Diahann Carol)

"The Great Gatsby" (Director: Jack Clayton, screenplay: FF Coppola – With Robert Redford and Mia Farrow)

MUSIC/DANCE

"Chelsea Hotel #2", by Leonard Cohen

David Bowie moves to the US, settles in New York

Opening of music club "The Bottom Line" on West 4th (Greenwich Village)

Release of "Celia & Johnny", by Salsa stars Johnny Pacheco and Celia Cruz (Vaya Records)

Concert by Melanie in Central Park

"*Pantomimes*", by Marcel Marceau (American tour)

TELEVISION/TV RELEASES

"Rhoda" (until 1978)

"Happy Days" (New York producer/director/actor/writer Garry Marshall's, with Ron Howard – Until 1984)

1975: <u>EVENTS</u>
End of the Vietnam war
Daily News headline on October 30: "Ford to City: Drop Dead"
Opening of "The Cockpit" leather store (bomber jackets and other stylized military apparel)
Andy Warhol's Mick Jagger series

<u>MOVIES:</u>
"Dog Day Afternoon" (Director: Sidney Lumet – With Al Pacino)
"Three Days of the Condor" (Director: Sidney Pollack – With Robert Redford, Faye dunaway)
"Hester Street" (Director: Joan Micklin Silver – With Steven Keats, Carol Kane)
"The Prisoner of Second Avenue" (Director: Melvin Frank – With Jack Lemmon and Anne Bancroft)

<u>MUSIC/DANCE</u>
Release of "Born to Run" (Bruce Springsteen)
Birth of Punk Rock at CBGB, with debuts from Talking Heads, Blondie, Patti Smith, The Ramones

<u>SPORTS</u>
Pelé signs 3-year contract with the New York Cosmos, becomes best paid athlete in the world

<u>TELEVISION/TV RELEASES</u>
"Saturday Night Live", with John Belushi, Gilda Radner, Dan Ackroyd, Chevy Chase – Bill Murray joins in 1976
"The Jeffersons", with Sherman Helmsley and Isabel Sanford (Until 1985)
"Welcome Back Kotter" with John Travolta and Gabe Kaplan (Until 1979)
"Barney Miller", with Hal Linden (until 1982)

<u>THEATRE/MUSICALS</u>
"A Chorus Line"
"The Sunshine Boys"
"The Wiz"

1976: UNDERLINE EVENTS
Bicentennial of the United States
Election of Jimmy Carter as President of the United States
Death of Carlo Gambino of natural causes – Replaced by Paul Castellano at the head of the New York Mafia
Serial murders by David Berkowitz ("The Son of Sam") – From January 1976 to August 1977
Closing of French hospital in Hells' Kitchen
Artist Frank Stella participates in Hervé Poulain's BMW Art Car Project

MOVIES:
"The Rocky Horror Picture Show" starts its midnight run at the Waverly Theatre. Audiences interact
"Next stop, Greenwich Village" (Director: Paul Mazursky – With Christopher Walken, Shelley Winters)
"King Kong" (Director: John Guillermin – With Jessica Lange, Jeff Bridges)
"Network" (Director: Sidney Lumet – With Peter Finch, Faye Dunaway, William Holden)
"Taxi Driver" (Director: Martin Scorsese, with Robert de Niro)
"Marathon Man" (Director: John Schlesinger – With Dustin Hoffman and Laurence Olivier)
"God Told Me To" (Director: Larry Cohen – With Tony Lo Bianco)
"The Blank Generation" (documentary on CBGB by Ivan Kral and Amos Poe)
"Next stop, Greenwich Village" (Director: Paul Mazursky – With Shelley Winters, Lenny Baker, Christopher Walken)

MUSIC
Concert by Bob Marley and the Wailers in Central Park
Release of "New York State of Mind" (Billy Joel & Tony Bennett)– also recorded by Barbra Streisand (1977)

RESTAURANTS
Reopening of "Tavern on the Green" after a $10-million renovation/ expansion
Opening of "Windows on the World" in the World Trade Center
Opening of "Hatsuhana" – First *Haute Cuisine* Japanese restaurant

TELEVISION/TV RELEASES
"Laverne and Shirley" (New York producer/director/actor/writer
  Garry Marshall, with Penny Marshall – until 1983)

THEATRE/MUSICALS
"Annie"
"Bubbling Brown Sugar"

1977: EVENTS
Jimmy Carter takes office
Andrew Young becomes the first black American Ambassador to the
  United Nations
Election of Democrat Ed Koch as Mayor of New York city, endorsed
  by both parties.
End of activist "Battling Bella" Abzug's political career
New York blackout (July 13 and 14)
Jimmy Coonan, last Irish American mobster, becomes the boss
  of the Westies organization, operating in Hell's Kitchen, in
  replacement of Mickey Spillane
David Berkowitz ("The Son of Sam") arrested (August 10)
Lufthansa heist at Kennedy Airport ($6 million, largest cash robbery
  in the US). John Gotti among the perpetrators.
Roy Lichtenstein participates in Hervé Poulain's BMW Art Car
  Project
Opening of swingers' club Plato's Retreat

MOVIES:
"Annie Hall" (Director: Woody Allen – With Woody Allen, Diane
  Keaton)
"Saturday Night Fever" (Director: John Badham – With John
  Travolta, Donna Pescow)
"New York, New York" (Director: Martin Scorsese – With Liza
  Minelli and Robert de Niro)
"The Goodbye Girl" (Director: Herbert Ross – With Richard
  Dreyfuss, Marsha Mason and Quinn Cummings)
"Thieves" (Director: John Berry – With Charles Grodin and Marlo
  Thomas)

MUSIC/DANCE
Release of "Psycho Killer" by Talking Heads
Opening of night club "Studio 54" (8th Avenue and 54th Street)
Captain Beef heart plays at The Bottom Line
Blondie, Talking Heads play at CBGB

SPORTS
New York Yankees win the World Series
New York Cosmos NASL champions – Record North American attendance: 77,691 at Giants' Stadium

1978: EVENTS
Renovation of the Commodore Hotel – First Manhattan project by Donald Trump
Death of Norman Rockwell
Isaac Bashevis Singer gets the Nobel Prize for Literature
Announcement of the resumption of work on the Cathedral of St. John the Divine

MOVIES:
The midnight run of "The Rocky Horror Picture Show" is taken over by the 8th Street Playhouse (Until 1992)
"Eraserhead" (by David Lynch) starts a two-year run at the Waverly Theater
Release of "Superman" (Director: Richard Donner – With Marlon Brando, Christopher Reeve, Gene hackman)

MUSIC/DANCE
Mikhail Baryshnikov joins the New York City Ballet
The Police play at CBGB
In December, Sid Vicious, of The Sex Pistols, is incarcerated on Rykers Island. He dies on his release in Feb. 1979

SPORTS:
New York Yankees win the World Series
New York Cosmos NASL soccer champions

TELEVISION/TV RELEASES
"Taxi", with Judd Hirsch, Danny de Vito, Andy Kaufman, Christopher Lloyd (Until 1983)

"Mork and Mindy" (New York producer/writer Garry Marshall, with Robin Williams – to 1982)

THEATRE/MUSICALS
Opening of "Ain't Misbehavin'"